# THE
# SEVENTH
# TOWER
## CASTLE

# THE SEVENTH TOWER
## CASTLE

GARTH NIX

HarperCollins *Children's Books*

First published in the USA by Scholastic Inc 2000
First published in Great Britain by HarperCollins *Children's Books* 2008
HarperCollins *Children's Books* is a division of HarperCollins*Publishers* Ltd,
77-85 Fulham Palace Road, Hammersmith, London W6 8JB

www.harpercollinschildrensbooks.co.uk

www.garthnix.co.uk

1

*The Seventh Tower : Castle*

ISBN 978 0 00 726120 8

Printed and bound in England by
Clays Ltd, St Ives plc

**Mixed Sources**
Product group from well-managed
forests and other controlled sources
www.fsc.org   Cert no. SW-COC-1806
© 1996 Forest Stewardship Council
FSC

FSC is a non-profit international organisation established to promote the
responsible management of the world's forests. Products carrying the FSC
label are independently certified to assure consumers that they come
from forests that are managed to meet the social, economic and
ecological needs of present and future generations.

Find out more about HarperCollins and the environment at
**www.harpercollins.co.uk/green**

*To my family and friends, with a particular thank you to everyone at Lucasfilm who has helped build and support The Seventh Tower, most particularly Sarah Hines Stephens, Jane Mason and Lucy Autrey Wilson.*

# 1

The Ruin Ship had rested in the foothills for many centuries. A vast hulk of bright metal that never rusted, it was the model that all the iceships of the Icecarls were patterned on, though theirs were made of Selski bone and hide.

Over time, luminous mosses and lichens had grown on the ship, so that its deck and sides glowed with soft light in many colours, rare in the eternal night of the Dark World. Even with its masts broken and its sails long gone, the Ruin Ship was enormous. It was easily five times the size of a typical clan ship, and they held a hundred Icecarls or more, with all their gear and cargo.

Tal, who until two weeks ago had thought there was nothing outside his home but ice, could not believe the strangely glowing shape ahead of him was a ship. He felt sure it was some freak of nature.

For all but fourteen days of his thirteen and three-quarter years, Tal had lived within the physical and social boundaries of the Castle. He had been raised to take his place among the Chosen, the masters of Light and Shadow. Like all Chosen, he had always been sure there was nothing beyond the light-filled halls and towers of the Castle. He had been taught that apart from the Chosen, there were only Underfolk, born to be servants.

No part of his life in the Castle had prepared him for the reality of the Ice, and the Icecarls who lived upon it. But the experience of surviving each day had chipped away his previously rock-solid beliefs. Tal was still a Chosen, as the shadowguard that stood at his side proclaimed. But his absolute belief in his natural superiority had been severely rattled.

He had even begun to accept that Icecarls were not Underfolk, even though they only had natural shadows. But he still held fast to the belief that the Chosen alone could make things of beauty and power. The Ruin Ship, which was both strangely beautiful and powerful, had to be some sort of natural phenomenon.

As the sleigh crawled higher up the icy slope, the six Wreska that pulled it had to work harder, their hot breath forming a constant cloud above their antlered heads, while their sharp X-toed hooves sprayed ice chips everywhere behind them.

"That's got to be a freak of ..." Tal muttered as the sleigh grew closer and the Ruin Ship loomed higher. His voice trailed off as his mind registered that this was not just a giant lump of wind-carved stone.

"What?" asked Milla, the Icecarl girl he'd been forced to travel across the ice with. She was sitting back and could barely see over the side of the sleigh.

"Nothing," replied Tal, shaking his head. A row of small stalactites broke off his face mask and flew toward Milla. But before they could hit, her hand moved in a blur of motion, batting them away.

"Don't shake your head," Milla instructed. "It's rude to shower ice on your companions."

Tal started to shrug, and even more ice fell off

his shoulders, more than Milla could bat away. She sighed and pulled her face mask down, an obvious snub.

Tal didn't care. The Icecarls made a big thing about showing or hiding their faces, but he really wasn't interested in mask etiquette. The wind was so cold that it seemed to go straight through his flesh, chilling his bones. Tal knew from bitter experience that without the mask, his teeth and cheekbones would quickly pick up a deep, internal ache that would last for hours.

Ignoring Milla, Tal looked ahead again. He had to accept that the Ruin Ship was constructed by humans. Even so, he stubbornly resisted the idea that the Icecarls had built it.

At the top of the ridge, the Icecarl who had been leading the Wreska halted for a few moments and turned the leaders toward a winding trail that was marked by luminous rocks, following the contour line down into darkness.

The ship was in a valley, the top of its broken masts level with the foothills of the Mountain of Light, the mountain on which the Castle was built.

As the sleigh jerked into motion again, Tal looked away from the ship and into the dark sky. Disoriented by the glow of the ship, he had to look up much higher than he expected before he saw the distant lights of the Castle.

The Castle was far bigger than the Ruin Ship, and its lights were the only brightness in the sky. Its seven towers even pierced the Veil, which shrouded the whole world from the sun.

Tal was comforted by the sight of his distant home. All his life he had been taught that only the Chosen mattered, that only the Chosen ever did anything or created anything worthwhile. The Castle was still the greatest structure in existence and this Ruin Ship of the Icecarls paled in comparison.

"Beautiful, isn't it?" Milla asked.

Tal looked back down. He'd never heard Milla say anything in such an awe-filled tone. For a moment he thought she'd finally accepted the importance of the Castle. Then he recognised that she had struggled up to look at the Ruin Ship.

"Shouldn't you be lying down?" he asked. Milla

had been badly wounded fighting a one-eyed Merwin, a vicious creature that from horn to tail had been longer than the sleigh and all six Wreska in front of it. Tal had managed to blind it with his Sunstone, but it was Milla who had killed the monster. Tal tried to remember that when she was being particularly obnoxious.

"It is the birthplace of our people," said Milla. "There are many tales of the ship. Many of our greatest sagas begin and end here."

She paused and took a breath that must have pained her, but she gave no sign of it before she declaimed:

> *"Green the ice glow, high on mast-head*
> *Black the blood, caked and ash-cold*
> *Red the ribbon, bound through beard*
> *White the Wreska, hauling him home*
> *Returns does Ragnar, dead many days."*

Tal didn't say anything. All of the Icecarls' poetry – or whatever it was – seemed to be about people who got themselves killed heroically on the Ice.

"The Ruin Ship is the chief place of the Shield Maidens," added Milla.

Now Tal understood why Millá had clawed herself up the side of the sleigh. The Shield Maidens roamed the Ice and settled disputes among the different clans, hunted down outlaws and killed dangerous creatures. As far as Tal could tell, the only people allowed to join were very scary women warriors with absolutely no sense of humour.

Milla kept staring at the Ruin Ship, ignoring the pain in her side. She had devoted her life to preparing herself to be a Shield Maiden. Icecarls measured their age in circlings, the time it took an iceship to complete one full circumnavigation of the world, following the continuous migration of the Selski.

From her fourth circling, as a small but ferocious child, Milla had worked unceasingly to be the best skater, to excel in the use of all weapons, to dare the most dangerous hunts.

Now, though she had only seen fourteen circlings, Milla was an exceptional fighter, even by the standards of her warrior race. She had proved it in her battle with the one-eyed Merwin.

There were few Icecarls who could have defeated the creature, even considering that Tal had blinded it with his Sunstone. This particular Merwin had been renowned for its viciousness and a full Hand of twelve Shield Maidens had been tracking it for many sleeps. They had come too late to fight the Merwin, but just in time to rescue Tal and the grievously wounded Milla.

Reluctantly, Milla looked down at the shadow that lay at Tal's feet. It looked normal enough now – but only because Tal had been warned that he would be killed if it behaved other than as an ordinary shadow. But she had seen it move by itself and take different shapes. Tal called it his shadowguard. Because Milla had shared Tal's blood in an oath-taking ritual, it had been able to take her shape and staunch her wounds until the Shield Maidens came.

She almost wished that it hadn't, for free-willed shadows were things of evil in Icecarl legend. Milla only hoped she would not be considered tainted by the shadow's touch, and so unfit to join the Shield Maidens.

As Milla was thinking of the Shield Maidens, Arla, the Shield Mother of the Hand, suddenly appeared out of the darkness. Without stopping to take off the thin, flat lengths of bone that she used to glide across the ice, she jumped on to the sleigh.

Tal flinched as she appeared. Arla was a stretch taller than him and the way she moved hinted at imminent violence. Her eyes were blue and as cold as the ice, and she never blinked when Tal was looking at her. She had horrific scars on her right arm that Milla said were from reaching into the gullet of an armour-skinned Krall to cut its throat from the inside.

Apart from the cold eyes, Arla was very beautiful behind her mask, with short golden hair that framed her oval face. Tal found the combination very disturbing.

"Only Shield Maidens may see the entrance to the Ruin Ship," Arla announced, pulling two long strips of soft Wreska skin out of one of the many pockets of her outer coat. "Tie these round your eyes as tight as you can. If you try to remove them, the punishment is death."

"Must I wear one, Shield Mother?" asked Milla. She had already taken the first step to being a novice Shield Maiden. In fact, the Quest that would make her a full Shield Maiden was to help Tal get back to the Castle – and find a new Sunstone for her clan ship.

"You are not yet a Shield Maiden," Arla observed. "Here we deal with what *is*, not with what *might* be."

Milla frowned, but didn't say anything. She took the blindfold and put it on. Tal put his on too. For a moment, he thought of slipping it up a bit so he could see. After all, he was a Chosen of the Castle and should not have to obey anyone here. But something about the way Arla had said "the punishment is death" encouraged him not to peek.

It was strange travelling on without being able to see anything, but Tal didn't mind being blindfolded as long as he knew there would be light when he took it off.

Even in the worst moments he'd spent outside the Castle, there had always been some light around Tal. Like his own Sunstone – now just a dead piece of rock since he'd used all its power to blind the Merwin. Milla's huge extended family, the clan of the Far Raiders, had had a Sunstone on its iceship, though it was fading. He'd even become used to the pallid green light of the Icecarls' moth-lanterns, like the ones on the sleigh.

Despite the fact that he was a prisoner of the Shield Maidens, Tal felt surprisingly secure. At least they would protect him from Merwin and rogue Selski and whatever other awful Ice creatures they might come across. Then, once he made it to the Ruin Ship, he was fairly sure that the Mother Crone of the Mountain of Light would believe his story and let him go home.

He felt a familiar anxiety as he thought of home. Anything could have happened to his family while he was gone. His father, Rerem, had disappeared. His mother, Graile, was very ill. His younger brother, Gref, had been captured by a Spiritshadow while following Tal as he climbed the outside of the Red Tower. And to make everything even more troubling, there were powerful Chosen in the Castle who were definitely Tal's enemies, though the boy didn't know why.

He had tried to tell himself that they weren't really enemies, just Chosen indulging bad temper or boredom. But deep down, he knew that wasn't so. He couldn't stop thinking about it, even though it made him feel slightly sick. He kept trying to think of reasons why someone would want him to dim down to the Red or make him an Underfolk. He deliberately avoided taking the consequences of that thought further.

After all, it was simply impossible that any Chosen would want his father never to return and his mother to die.

"I have to get back," he whispered to himself. Milla rustled at his side and he knew that she must have heard him. Tal bit his lip, wishing he hadn't spoken. Milla would just think he was being weak.

"Quiet," snapped Arla. Tal flinched. He hadn't realised the Shield Mother was still in the sleigh with them. She was so quiet. All of them were.

They travelled in silence for some time, the sleigh going down into the valley. Finally, it stopped. Tal could hear the Wreska being unharnessed and led away, their sharp X-toed hooves distinctive on the ice.

"Take my hand," instructed Arla, pushing her hand around Tal's. "Milla, you will be carried."

"I can walk!" Milla protested, though Tal knew she could barely sit up. The Merwin horn had cut her whole side open, and though the Shield Maidens had healed the actual wound very rapidly – with a treatment of foul-smelling ointment and weird, rhythmic chanting – Milla had still lost an awful lot of blood and was very weak.

Tal closed his hand, clumsy in its thick fur glove, around Arla's and let her lead him out of the sleigh. At first they walked on ice, with Tal slipping and sliding, and Arla completely balanced.

Then Arla said, "Ware steps!" and Tal's bone-nailed boots were no longer crunching on ice, but on something else. His footsteps let out a deep hollow clang, as if he trod on a metal plate. Tal was surprised – he hadn't seen the Icecarls use metal like this before. Everything they had was made of stone or bone, skin, gut, teeth, and other bits and pieces of animals.

Still, the sound continued. The wind that had blown around them suddenly cut off too – they must have entered some sort of shelter. Perhaps they were already inside the ship… .

Tal put out his free hand and touched an entirely smooth surface, too smooth to be anything but highly worked stone or wood... or metal. He tapped it and heard another dull ringing sound. He would have done the same on the other side, but Arla still held his hand in a grip he could not evade.

The noise changed again and the ground felt softer under Tal's feet. Almost like the grass that grew in the garden caverns of the Chosen. But surely it was too cold for anything to grow here, even out of the wind?

They kept walking, with sudden changes of direction that totally confused Tal. Every now and then he was spun around several times, and made to climb up and down steps.

Tal desperately wanted to see, but he made no move towards his blindfold. It wasn't worth the risk.

Finally, they stopped. Arla let go of his hand and then Tal felt fingers at the back of his head, undoing the blindfold. Light streamed in and he blinked.

He was in a large, perfectly rectangular room. The walls and ceiling were a deep golden metal, polished enough so that he could see his own reflection. The floor was covered in a thick carpet of stitched-together squares of fur.

There was a Merwin horn in each corner of the room. Each horn had a Sunstone set on its tip, filling the room with bright, even light. In such light, there could be no shadows – save for Tal's shadowguard, which was doing its best to be small and stay close to its master's heels.

A long table of yellow bone stood in the middle of the room, loaded with knives, pots, a pile of wet and rubbery vegetable roots, and a large chunk of pale pink meat. A very old woman was cutting the meat into paper-thin slices with a sharp knife made of the same golden metal as the walls. It was the first metal knife Tal had seen since leaving the Castle.

It wasn't until he looked up from the hypnotic rise and fall of the knife that Tal noticed the old woman had the same milky eyes as the Mother Crone on the Far Raiders' ship. She had to be blind, though she didn't wield the knife as if she were.

It chopped up and down with the rhythm of Tal's own heart, cutting perfect slices of almost see-through meat without endangering her fingers.

There was only one other person in the room. A younger Crone, sitting on a stool in the corner. She looked at Tal and he saw the liquid silver flash of her eyes. All the Crones were very creepy. If they didn't have milky eyes, they had these unnaturally bright ones, which seemed to look right inside him.

As well as cutting the meat without difficulty, the milky-eyed Crone also seemed to know who was there. Without stopping her cutting, she looked across and said, "Arla. You have brought our visitors. Welcome to the Ruin Ship, Milla and Tal."

She raised her blade and the metal flashed in the light.

"I've been expecting you," added the Crone, bringing the knife slashing back down.

"We greet you, Mother Crone," said Milla, clapping her clenched fists together. Tal reached for his Sunstone to give light as a sign of respect, then remembered that it was dead. He quickly bowed his head instead.

The Mother Crone stopped cutting the meat and wrapped several slices with strands of a black vegetable. She put the resulting parcels on plates of translucent bone.

"Come, eat," she said. "We will talk."

There were no chairs, so Tal and Milla approached the table. Arla and the other Crone on the stool didn't move. Obviously the invitation didn't apply to them.

Tal looked down at his plate and wished the invitation didn't apply to him either. Not only was the meat raw, the black stuff wasn't a vegetable he recognised. It was wet, for a start, and looked sticky. He closed his eyes and swallowed the lump all in one mouthful. It went down so quickly he hardly tasted it.

"A rare treat," the Mother Crone said with a smile that made the wrinkles around her clouded eyes stand out even more. "Kerusk fish and seaweed, from under the Ice."

"Under the Ice?" Tal blurted out. How could you get under the Ice? He could understand catching fish by cutting a hole where the ice was thin and using a hook and line, but how would you harvest this seaweed?

"We have our ways," said the Mother Crone. "Now I wish to see your shadow, Tal."

"It's there," said Tal nervously, pointing down to where his shadowguard lay next to Milla's feet. It seemed a bit silly pointing out his shadow to a blind woman.

"No," said the Mother Crone. "I wish to see it walk without you."

She sounded quite stern now. Tal looked at her, wondering how her milky eyes could possibly see anything. Or perhaps the Mother Crone had another means of perceiving things?

"Shadowguard, shadowguard," he whispered, after a glance at Arla and Milla. "Make me a shape, as meek as you can."

As he spoke, the shadowguard lost its boy shape and slowly shifted into something else. A Dattu, Tal was relieved to see. A large, innocuous rodent that lived in the grassy hills of Aenir, the spirit world of the Chosen.

"Beware the shadow that walks alone," muttered Arla. She had seen the shadowguard help Milla stay alive after the Merwin attack. But after that, the Shield Mother had warned Tal that he would die if his shadow left him for an instant.

If the threat hadn't been so serious, Tal would have laughed. The Icecarls might be a cut above the Underfolk in some ways, but not by much. If they knew how to use Sunstones properly they wouldn't worry about a shadowguard like Tal's. He doubted they *could* learn how to use Sunstones properly, since that required concentrated thought. As far as Tal could see, Icecarls weren't deep thinkers. They acted on instinct, usually with violence.

"This is not one of those shadows," said the Mother Crone. "It is a lesser thing, still in its infancy. The ones we should fear cannot change their shape."

"Spiritshadows?" asked Tal, unable to suppress a superior smile. Even though he'd had some bad experiences with Spiritshadows, they were still only the tools of the Chosen who had mastered them. "They're only servants, like the Underfolk. Each is bound to obey its Master. No Chosen would set a Spiritshadow against you. What would be the point? There is nothing out here that would interest a real Chosen. I mean, no one has ever bothered to see if there was anything out here before, and even when they do find out, I don't think they will be interested..."

His voice trailed off. It was hard to explain without being totally rude.

"Perhaps," said the Mother Crone. "Yet we have long known about your Castle and its seven

Towers. And both Chosen and Shadows have come down from the mountain before."

Tal was silent. He didn't know what to say to that. The Mother Crone was probably trying to impress him and he doubted she really knew anything about the Castle and the Chosen. Nothing important anyway.

"All I want is to get home," he muttered when the Mother Crone didn't say any more. "I have to get back and get a Sunstone!"

"Two Sunstones," he added, a split second after Milla looked at him, her eyes as sharp as knives. "One for the Far Raiders as well."

"Yes," said the Mother Crone. She took the knife and plunged it deep into the slab of meat in front of her, making Tal jump back. Milla didn't even flinch. "But in all the time that the Ruin Ship has been here, and the Shield Maidens have patrolled these hills, we have never let anyone climb the Mountain of Light, the source of Shadow. Why should we let *you* pass?"

Tal looked down at the floor as he struggled to think of a reason that would seem important to these Icecarls. But nothing came. No brilliant words. No clever answers. Just one truth.

"It's my home," Tal said miserably. "It's where I belong."

"Yes," said the Mother Crone. "To the ship comes the Icecarl, home from the Ice, while the Chosen goes home to the Castle."

She walked around the table and stood close to Tal. She seemed taller, closer up, a good head taller than Tal. She only wore light furs and her arms were bare, showing many scars. Closer up, the milkiness in her eyes seemed more like the luminous glow of the moth-lamps than the result of age or illness.

From the scars, Tal guessed that the Mother Crone had once been a fierce Shield Maiden. She still had a forbidding menace when she wanted to.

"How can we return you without opening a way back to us, a way that Shadows may seek to use?"

"I don't know," said Tal. "But the Mother Crone of the Far Raiders said I would go back. Didn't she?"

He directed that question at Milla, who had heard the other Mother Crone's strange prophesy. But it was *this* Mother Crone who answered.

"*Home is the Castle, Yet it is not home,*" she recited, repeating two lines of the prophecy. "Even among Crones, the truth of what we see is not always clear. Tell me, Shield Mother, what do you think we should do with Tal?"

"Give him to the Ice," said Arla, without expression.

"What?!" exclaimed Tal. That was the same as killing him.

"And you, Milla?" asked the Mother Crone. "What should we do with this boy who is bound to your Quest?"

"Mother Crone, the Far Raiders do need a Sunstone," said Milla. Tal looked at her gratefully, but she didn't meet his eyes.

"As do the Selski Runners and the Sharp Spears and the South Corner, among many others," replied the Mother Crone. "Many others. Too many. So we shall not be giving you to the Ice, Tal. Not while you can be useful."

"How?" asked Tal, though he could guess.

"Sunstones," said the Mother Crone. "The old ones fail, and though some are found, they do not last as long. Why do the Sunstones that fall to us fade so quickly? We do not know. That, and other things, trouble us. The clans need Sunstones. The Crones need knowledge. So we have decided that perhaps we will let you return to your Castle. Come."

She turned away and went over to a wall, pulling down a curtain of patchwork furs to reveal an open doorway. "You too, Milla. Shield Mother, you may leave us."

*Perhaps*, Tal thought, was often only a way of saying *no*. But this time, he thought it meant *yes*. Only, knowing the Icecarls, there was bound to be some sort of catch. He'd already been forced into swearing he'd get a Sunstone for the Far Raiders. Maybe the Mother Crone would want one too.

But then Tal would swear to anything, anything at all, in order to get home. He'd worry about the consequences later.

The Crone Mother led Milla and Tal along a short corridor, into a huge chamber that Tal realised must once have been the main hold of the ship.

A vast area, it was not well-lit, and what light there was seemed to come from a mixture of Sunstones, moth-lamps and glowjellies – an odd combination of colour and illumination. To make it even stranger, Tal couldn't work out exactly where all the light was coming from.

Most of the room was filled with what looked like a very strange playing board. As Tal paced along behind the Crone, he estimated the board had to be eighty stretches long and forty wide, since one of his paces was roughly equivalent to a stretch.

The board – or whatever it was – occupied the entire middle section of the hold. Peering at it in the dim light, Tal saw that it was made up of many thousands of square tiles. There were twenty or thirty slipper-wearing Icecarls moving around on it, shifting small models of iceships or, not quite so frequently, rearranging the tiles with different ones they brought to the board.

The Icecarls were all girls around Milla's age, which Tal guessed was close to his own – a bit under fourteen.

They all wore indoor furs of the same white colour, with similar patterns of black bars. Tal didn't know what sort of animal the furs came from. It wasn't the black, shiny Selski hide used in Milla's armour or the soft brown Wreska skin that lined his own gloves, and he hadn't seen the black-and-white pattern on any other Icecarls. Arla's Shield Maidens wore black Selski-hide breastplates, bracers and greaves over white furs striped with silver.

The girls were under the direction of seven women, who sat in high-backed chairs of woven bone located at even intervals around the enormous playing board.

The women were Crones, Tal guessed. At least they all had the same telltale glow in their eyes, like the Crone of the Far Raiders, or the woman who had sat in the background when they met the Crone Mother. Tal wondered how their eyes got so bright and what happened to them when they became Mother Crones to make their eyes change again.

The seven Crones seemed to be looking out into space, but every now and then one would crook her finger, and a girl would lightly cross the board and go to her. There would be a whispered conversation, then the girl would go back to the board and move a ship, or perhaps exchange one of the tiles, taking a replacement from one of a number of cabinets that lined the far wall.

As they walked closer, the girls stopped whatever they were doing to acknowledge the Mother Crone by clapping their fists. When she stopped at the edge of the board, Tal went over to get a closer look. He saw that every tile was etched with faintly luminous symbols. Doing a quick estimation, Tal calculated that there were around fourteen hundred tiles and four or five hundred ship models.

He also saw that at the very centre of the board there was one model that was not a ship. It was a mountain, with a building on top of it. A building with seven towers that glowed with tiny Sunstone chips. Clearly it was the Castle and the Mountain of Light. Below it was a model of the Ruin Ship, covered in the same luminous lichens that grew on the real thing.

"It's a map," Tal said suddenly. Each tile represented a certain area – he had no idea how big – and the symbols on it indicated the terrain, or perhaps the state of the Ice. Each model was also unique, representing a different Icecarl clan and ship.

Tal looked at Milla. She was staring at the girls with obvious longing. They had to be Shield Maiden cadets who had fulfilled their Quest and begun their training. They were what Milla wanted to be, with all her heart.

"We call it the Reckoner. It is a map of sorts," said the Mother Crone. "Look closely at the ships, Tal."

He peered at some of the closer ones. They were carved out of translucent bone, or maybe stone. The light actually came from inside the vessels. Some were filled with luminous moths, some with glowjellies and some with a tiny Sunstone fragment. Tal wasn't sure what this meant, but fewer than forty in a hundred ships were lit by Sunstones.

"Once, nearly every clan had a Sunstone," said the Mother Crone. "Now it is as you see."

"How do you know?" asked Tal. Then he looked at the girls, moving ships from one tile to the next. "You mean this... Reckoner actually shows where all the ships are right *now*, and whether they've got a Sunstone?"

"*And* the conditions of the Ice," Milla added, staring at the table with rapt attention. "Among other things."

"But how?" Tal asked, alarmed. If there really were that many ships, there were far more Icecarls than he'd suspected. And they must have powerful magic to know where every ship was!

"What one Crone sees, all may see, waking or sleeping," said the Mother Crone. "And all clans have at least one Crone. We Icecarls are not without power, Tal. Remember that when you return to the Castle."

"I'll remember," said Tal quickly. But he wasn't really concerned with Icecarl magic. He'd just heard words that were much more magical to him than Crones who could see through one another's eyes. *When you return to the Castle.*

"But when can I go? And how do I get there?"

"This ship is not the only ruin that can be found on the Mountain of Light," the Mother Crone answered. "There was once a road that went from base to crown. Most of it has long since crumbled and it no longer goes anywhere near the top. But even ruined, it will make your way easier, until you can enter the Castle by other ways."

"Other ways?"

Tal didn't like the sound of that. It made getting back to the Castle sound difficult, but even worse was the thought that the Icecarls might know secret ways into his home. To cover up how disturbed he was, he scratched under his eye, covering his expression with his hand.

"I am not sure exactly what or where these ways are, but I know they exist," said the Mother Crone. She walked away from the Reckoner and went to one of the cabinets, her fingers gently touching items on several shelves. Tal and Milla followed her, Milla still half watching the girls who moved the ships and tiles.

"Ah, this is it," said the old woman, taking a small and very dusty bag of Selski hide off the shelf and handing it to Tal. "Open it."

Tal opened the bag, sneezing as dust billowed from inside. There were two objects in there: a thin rectangle of bone no larger than his hand, and a magnifying glass with a gold rim.

"Long ago," the Mother Crone began, "when I was a little older than one of these young Shield Maidens, a man was found near the Ruin Ship – a man without a shadow. He had lost it, he said, and perhaps he had, though we noticed that he was afraid of *all* shadows, as if his own might return. He called himself a Chosen, from the Castle of Seven Towers, though he would say no more. We did not ask him to explain, for he was not the first stranger to come down the Mountain of Light. The memory of the Crones is long.

"He stayed with us for many sleeps, carving away at that bone, using this glass to keep his work smaller and more secret. He never said exactly what it was, but I think it is a map, showing a way into your Castle."

Tal looked at the tablet of bone with more interest and raised the magnifying glass to his eye. It was a strong one, so even in the bad light he could make out tiny drawings etched into the surface. There were characters there too, writing so fine that it must have been carved with the sharpest of needles. Tal needed better light to see what it said, though the alphabet was the one commonly used in the Castle, not the more complex runes used in the spirit world of Aenir.

"Did he tell you his name?" asked Tal. "What happened to him?"

"We called him Longface, for when he first came his eyebrows and much of his hair had been burned off, so that his forehead was tall and as smooth as his chin. After he finished that carving he grew weak and could not be healed. We gave him to the Ice."

Tal shuddered. The Icecarls were too keen to put anyone weak or useless out on to the Ice. Tal had seen no old Icecarls, except for the Crones.

"You may have Longface's map," said the Mother Crone, "and any other supplies you need. Milla will have to rest for several days before you can go on, but after that, you are free to leave. If Milla returns with her Sunstone, we will know that the time has come for Icecarls and Chosen to meet. If not, we shall look for other ways to find our knowledge ... and our Sunstones."

There was no menace in her voice, but Tal felt that this was a veiled threat. At first, he wasn't worried about it. The Icecarls were fierce and the Crones obviously had powers he did not understand, but they could never stand up to the Light magic of the Chosen and the strength of their Spiritshadows.

But as he thought about it, Tal looked out at the Reckoner again, and all the ships. There were an awful lot of them, perhaps close to five hundred. Spread all over the world, fortunately... but they greatly outnumbered the Chosen. If they could get into the Castle...

"Milla doesn't have to come," he said. "I could bring a Sunstone back."

"You would return here?" asked the Mother Crone, with a faint hint of a smile. "I think it best if Milla does go with you and finds a Sunstone herself."

"Sure," said Tal unhappily. He'd got used to travelling with Milla when she was wounded – and quiet. He wasn't sure about travelling with her once she was healthy. He never knew what she was going to do and he suspected that she would still like to kill him. In her mind, he had never been more than a trespasser who'd come up with a good excuse to save himself.

Still, she had sworn an oath. He could probably trust her – at least until they got to the Castle. Then Tal would have a whole new set of troubles...

For the next four days and five sleeps, Tal tried to roam around the Ruin Ship. But whenever he went to open a hanging curtain or go through a doorway, one of the Shield Maiden cadets would pop up from behind, or in front, or from around the corner, and politely lead him back to somewhere he'd already been.

Eventually he worked out that he was only allowed to be in the small sleeping chamber he'd been assigned, the Hall of the Reckoner, the Cadets' Feasting Hall where he had his meals (though he never saw anything he'd call a feast) and, some of the time, the room where Milla had been ordered to stay in bed.

The only combat skill Milla could practise in bed was her bad temper. Since Tal was the only person she could practise on and get away with it, he found that visiting her was not much fun. But there was simply nothing else to do, except watch the ships and tiles get moved around on the Reckoner, and that was about as boring as the lecture on the basics of light that retired Lector Jannem gave every year.

On the positive side, though she was cross at being ordered to bed, Milla was bored too, and sometimes she would actually answer Tal's questions. The Shield Maiden cadets wouldn't speak to him at all, unless it was to stop him from going somewhere or doing something he wasn't allowed to do.

"How come there are no men here?" Tal asked Milla on the second day, after he'd ducked a pillow she'd thrown at him. He handed it back to her, noting that her face had lost its sickly grey tinge and was returning to its normal, surprisingly delicate paleness. All the Icecarls were very pale, much more so than the Chosen.

Most Icecarls had the same colour hair, too, like sunshine mixed with white ash. Tal's hair was the colour of dirt, settling just above his shoulders. He felt that cutting his hair short would be an admission that he was no longer a proper Chosen.

"No men where?" snarled Milla.

"Here, the Ruin Ship."

"I told you," snapped Milla. "It is the chief place of the Shield Maidens. It is not like a normal clan ship. There are no families, no children, no hunters, no Selski. The only men who come here would be either lost hunters, messengers... or a Sword Thane."

"A Sword Thane?" asked Tal, suddenly interested.

"Women who wish to serve all the clans become Shield Maidens," explained Milla. "But men do not work so well together, so those who wish to be lawgivers and protectors become Sword Thanes."

"What do you mean?" asked Tal.

"Everyone knows this." Milla frowned. "Some clans prefer a Sword Thane, though they can be unreliable and hard to find. It makes a better saga, I suppose."

"Prefer a Sword Thane for what?"

"Trouble!" spat Milla. "When you have trouble, you send for the Shield Maidens, but sometimes a Sword Thane finds you and the trouble first."

"But aren't Shield Maidens heroes?" Tal asked. "I mean, you killed the Merwin. Doesn't that make you a hero – which makes you a Sword Thane?"

"I wish to be a Shield Maiden, so I must try to be a hero," Milla repeated. "But only a man can be a Sword Thane. All Sword Thanes are heroes but not all heroes are Sword Thanes."

"What?" asked Tal. He was getting confused. "So what do you call a man who's a hero but not a Sword Thane? What if he uses an axe or a spear?"

Milla didn't answer. She picked up the Merwin horn sword that never left her side and readied it to throw like a spear. Tal didn't stay to be a target, or for further explanation about Shield Maidens and Sword Thanes. He disappeared around the corner and did not visit Milla again till she was up, and final preparations were being made for their departure.

They left the Ruin Ship after a stay of a full five

sleeps, the same way they had entered, stumbling along blindfolded, guided by Arla. This time at least they were much better equipped. The Shield Maidens had been generous in providing new furs, climbing teeth, ropes of braided Selski hide and other things they considered essential to climb the ruined road to the Mountain of Light.

Tal had used part of the time in the ship to study Longface's map. He had come to the conclusion that the bone had not actually been carved with a sharp tool, but cut by Sunstone light. That meant the Chosen who had done it had been extremely skilled and that he still had his Sunstone when he had staggered down to the Ruin Ship. But not his Spiritshadow.

The tablet gave no clue to its maker's mystery. There was writing on it, in addition to regular marks that were obviously a map. But all the writing said was: *Half road down pyramid Imrir fallen 100 stretch entry heatway tunnel Underfolk 7.*

Tal had puzzled over this for some time, but all he could guess was that it meant there was an entrance to the heating system of the Castle – which he knew went through the mountain, right down into the deep earth. *Underfolk 7* was almost certainly a reference to the lowest of the Underfolk levels, which Tal supposed was where the heatway tunnel came out. Presumably the entrance outside would be about halfway up the mountain, near a fallen pyramid.

Tal had a dim recollection that Imrir had been the Emperor long ago. The current Empress didn't have a name – Tal had never wondered about that before. Of course, she had been the Empress for much longer than most, fending off old age with her mastery of Sunstone magic. Maybe Emperors's or Empresses's names were only known after they died.

All thoughts of the Empress were gone by the time the blindfold came off. Arla left them, without a word. Tal watched with relief as she silently slid away. He felt like a caveroach about to be stepped on when Arla was around. Milla, of course, had a completely different reaction. Arla was everything Milla wanted to be twenty circlings from now.

Tal stood alone with Milla and the freezing

wind. Far below, they could see the luminous outline of the Ruin Ship.

Both of them had moth-lanterns, but the dull green light only showed snow and patches of bare rock. If there was a road – even a ruined one – Tal couldn't see it.

"Come on," ordered Milla. She shouldered her pack and headed off. Tal fumbled on his own pack, groaning at the sudden weight. It was full of sleeping furs and climbing gear and food and what felt like at least his own weight in other things the Icecarls considered essential. Tal would have rather had a Sunstone, so he could properly warm himself. Even with inner and outer coats of thick fur, a cloth-lined bone face mask and a short, hooded cape lined with the soft tails of something he couldn't pronounce, Tal was still cold.

Though he couldn't see a road through the amber lenses of his mask, he followed obediently. Either Milla could see something, or Arla had told her a secret sign to look for.

It was hard going, but not *too* hard. At times they had to clamber over great blocks of ice that had slid down from higher up, but it was clear they were on a path made by humans.

Once again, Tal regretted the absence of a Sunstone. He wanted to light up the whole mountainside, to see the sheer cliffs stretching up and up, and admire the way the rock had been carved away in precise lines to create the road, zigzagging its way up what would otherwise be impassable terrain.

But all he could see now was the occasional evidence of construction, particularly when there was a well-preserved stretch of road and mountainside forming a perfect right angle. At other times, he had no idea how Milla found the road again after it had fallen away. He asked her.

"The road smells of ghalt, the melting stone," Milla said. As usual, her voice bore a reluctance to talk to Tal, tempered with a desire to show off how superior Icecarls were. She bent down, swept away a light layer of snow and, with effort, pulled out a piece of black rock that shone in the moth-light.

"There are hot pools of ghalt in the far southern mountains," she said, holding the piece under Tal's nose. "When it is hot it pours like water and smells very sour. Even very old, cold ghalt smells. I do not know how the ancients brought it here for the road."

Tal raised his mask to sniff at it, but he couldn't smell anything. His face just got cold. As the hours of walking wore on, Tal was no longer interested in how Milla found the road. He was just glad that she did. He was also hoping that she would stop soon so he could rest. She had to be tired too, he reasoned, since she was still recovering from her wound. But she showed no signs of weariness.

When she did stop, it wasn't for a rest. She suddenly backed up, almost hitting Tal. While he gawped at her, she threw her arm around him and wrestled him into the nearest snowdrift, piled up against the mountainside.

As they plunged into the snow, Tal felt a great rush of air go past. He caught a momentary glimpse of enormous translucent eyes, each as large as his own head, followed by spread wings of great size.

"What was that?"

Milla clapped her hand over his mouth, her fur

glove almost smothering Tal. He started to struggle, then stopped as she held a knife against his throat and ordered him in a whisper, "Stay still!"

They lay together in the snow, not moving. Finally, they heard a terrible screech some distance off and Milla relaxed. The knife vanished from her hand and she let Tal sit up.

"Perawl," she said. "They can't see you if you stay completely still. They're a bit deaf as well."

"What was the... the noise?" asked Tal. The unseen hunters in the air made this place even worse than being on the Ice. At least with the Selski you could hear them coming, and you could see a Merwin's luminous horn. Milla didn't answer, so Tal repeated the question.

"It could be any one of a number of things," replied Milla evasively. "The Perawl's meal, I suppose."

"So the great Milla doesn't know everything," remarked Tal. Milla ignored him, her attention still focused downhill.

"Perhaps... perhaps it was the other way around," Tal added. The screech hadn't sounded like something being caught. It had sounded triumphant.

"Maybe the Perawl was something else's meal."

They looked at each other, expressions unseen behind their face masks. But Milla started off again at a faster pace and Tal followed without complaint.

Without his Sunstone, Tal had no idea how much later it was when they finally stopped to rest and eat. As on the Ice, the meal was Selski meat heated over a Selski oil stove.

"We will have three watches. I will take the first and third," declared Milla when they had finished eating. "You need only stay awake for the middle watch."

"I can stand two watches," said Tal. "Let's have four watches."

"Do you know how to count every breath without thinking, even while asleep?" asked Milla.

"Uh, no," answered Tal. "What does—"

"That is how we count the passing time when there is no other means," explained Milla, as if she were speaking to a very small child. "So I will tell you when to begin and finish your watch."

Tal couldn't argue with that. Surreptitiously, he tried to count each individual breath, but he couldn't keep track. He half suspected that Milla couldn't either and she was just trying to be superior again.

It was a cold camp, and a dangerous one, with a long drop beside the road. They put their backs against the slope and Tal silently told himself thirty times, *I must not walk in my sleep.*

Sleep did not come easily. The wind howled down the mountain and seemed to want to pick Tal and Milla up and take them with it all the way to the Ruin Ship far below. Because they were higher up, it was even colder than on the Ice, and Tal found himself huddling closer and closer to Milla to stay warm.

Milla seemed to take this as normal behaviour, but Tal found even her fur-muffled closeness unnerving. He had never been so close to a girl before, let alone one who might kill him if he accidentally threw his arm around her while he was dreaming.

That thought didn't help him sleep. Neither did the noises he heard, or thought he heard, in the night. Even when Milla was supposed to be sleeping, she sat up every now and then to listen. Sometimes Tal wondered if she ever really slept.

He wouldn't have been surprised to find that if she did sleep, it was with one eye open.

The middle watch seemed to go on and on forever. Tal decided to test if Milla was asleep. He leaned away from her, but she didn't stir. So he edged away a little more. She sank back into her furs and Tal smiled. She really was asleep.

He reached across to lightly tickle under her chin, where a tiny square of skin showed clear of the mask and her laced-up collar. Tal had often done this to Gref, trailing his fingernail like an insect across him to see how long it took for his brother to wake up.

His gloved hand was just about to touch Milla's chin when her hand snaked out from under the sleeping furs her knife held at roughly the same point under Tal's chin. For a frozen moment they faced each other, then Tal slowly withdrew his hand and Milla her knife.

"Two hundred and seventy-five breaths," said Milla. "I will know when it is my turn."

Tal was very wakeful for the rest of his watch, but sleep claimed him quickly when Milla took over.

Despite this, he felt like he'd had no sleep at all when Milla shook him awake and they started off again. This time, the climbing became harder, as more of the road had been destroyed by avalanches. In some places the mountain had simply slipped away. They had to climb up very steep slopes of ice and stone, using ropes, Wreska jawbones full of sharp teeth strapped on to the sides of their boots, and bone spikes – called pitons – hammered in with a rounded stone as big as Tal's fist.

Milla was an experienced climber. Tal was not. Luckily he had his shadowguard to help, though he tried not to call on it too much. He didn't want Milla to think he was beholden to his shadow.

Tal's greatest difficulty was not being able to see. When climbing, the moth-lanterns had to be strapped to their backpacks, so most of the light fell behind them rather than in front.

It was even worse when it snowed. The first two "days" (by Milla's reckoning) stayed clear and cold. But halfway through their second sleep, the snow came down heavily, so much that they would have been buried under it if they'd been on level ground.

The snow kept up through their third day, then just as Tal was falling asleep, turned into particularly wet and unpleasant sleet that came in sudden bursts, blowing horizontally in wet sheets that soaked the travellers' outer coats in an instant. Fortunately, the inner furs stayed dry, evidence of the Icecarls' long practice of living in the wild.

By this stage, Tal was so tired that as soon as Milla told him he could sleep, he slept, no matter what the weather was doing.

On the fourth day, the sleet finally faltered and then stopped altogether. The wind died down too, and the air became still. They made faster progress and within a few hours they came to something that had to be the fallen pyramid mentioned on the bone tablet.

They first saw it when it reflected their lights, and for a heart-stopping instant, both thought themselves face-to-face with the eyes of some huge creature. But as the reflection multiplied, it became clear that what lay ahead was not a living thing.

Trudging wearily up the road, they saw that it was a pyramid. A pyramid of blue crystal, three times as tall as Milla. It must have slid down the mountain long ago, because it no longer stood upright. The point now angled back into the mountain, rather than up at the dark sky.

"The entry to the heatway tunnel must be close," said Tal. "Within a hundred stretches, the tablet says."

"Does it mention *that*?" asked Milla, raising her lantern. The green light spilled forward and reflections from the pyramid swam back.

Right in front of the pyramid the road simply wasn't there any more. It had fallen away, leaving a frightening gap.

"Oh," said Tal. "No, it doesn't."

Cautiously, Tal and Milla crept to the edge. They could not see any bottom.

"Can we climb up and over?" asked Tal, looking at the mountainside.

Milla moved her lantern across, noting the loose rock and signs of recent slippage. Then she shook her head.

"The rock face is too loose," she announced. "We will have to jump the gap."

"Jump?" exclaimed Tal. "Impossible. It must be ten… even twelve stretches!"

Milla tilted her face mask back and looked at the chasm again. "No, we can jump it," she said. "Even you."

"There has to be another way," Tal said desperately. He went over to the side of the road against the mountain and tested his weight against an outcropping of rock above his head.

The rock came free, with a lot more besides, nearly braining Tal. Milla was right. It was too loose. Tal looked down at the gap again. It would be suicide to try to jump over it. He couldn't even see the bottom. They were almost at a turn in the road, so it would be a straight drop to the road below. That had to be at least five hundred stretches!

He looked back. Milla was strapping the toothy jawbones they used as spikes on to her boots. She had also taken out something Tal hadn't seen before. Gloves of thin Selski hide, with long curved claws of reddish bone.

"You will have to help me with the claw-hands," Milla said as she finished strapping on her boot-teeth. She then tried to hammer a bone piton into the road, but it wouldn't go through the sections where there was metal and the stone crumbled everywhere else.

Finally, Milla shrugged and put the piton back. She left her pack lying on the ground and strapped her Merwin-horn sword on to her back instead. She slipped on the clawed gloves. Tal saw that they had to be tied on to her wrists, so he helped her, patiently following her instructions on how to do the right knots.

"Move the lanterns to the edge," said Milla. She had not put her mask back on. Tal saw her eyes move calculatingly to the far edge.

"Shouldn't you be tied to a rope?" he asked. "I could hold it…"

"There is nothing to secure it to," said Milla. "You would only be dragged down."

She hesitated, then said, "If I fail, Tal, you will try to go on? You will fulfill the Quest and get a Sunstone for my clan? Then I may become a Shield Maiden, even after death."

Tal looked at the dark gap and was tempted to say that if Milla couldn't jump it, he would have no chance. But she had used his name and hadn't looked at him with her usual scorn. "I will try," he said with a gulp.

"I would not ask, normally," said Milla. "But I am still not at my full strength."

"Great," Tal muttered under his breath. He looked at the gap again, then reached out to touch Milla's claw-hands.

"All right, I'll jump first," he said.

"What?" Milla was suddenly angry again. "Do you doubt my courage?" She took her hands away and stalked back twenty or so steps, out of the light of the lanterns. "I'll show you a Shield Maiden's courage!" she shouted angrily.

"No, Milla!" shouted Tal. "Wait! I didn't mean... take your time —"

Before he could finish, Milla came sprinting out of the darkness. She passed Tal in a blur, her arms and legs pumping. Two paces from the edge, she threw herself forward, arms outstretched.

"Yaaaahhhhhhhh!"

Tal rushed to the edge. There was a clatter of rocks. He couldn't see Milla on the other side. He raised one of the lanterns, a sick feeling in his stomach.

Nothing moved in the small pool of light.

"Milla!" Tal shouted, his voice echoing into the emptiness. No answer came, but one small movement caught Tal's eye. A clawed hand, reaching up over the lip on the far side.

Another followed it, then Milla's head. With a choking grunt, she pulled herself up over the edge and crawled a few paces forward. Anyone normal would have collapsed gratefully then, but Milla staggered to her feet and looked back at Tal.

As their eyes met, Tal realised that now he had

to jump. Without the claw-hands. But at least there was no wind.

"Throw over a rope," Milla yelled. "I will secure it to the pyramid."

Tal rummaged out a rope with relief. At least he would have a rope. If he did fall, it would only be… well, far enough to be seriously hurt instead of killed. If he was lucky.

When he turned to throw the rope over to Milla, she was bent over, her hands on her knees, obviously in pain. As soon as he moved, she shot back upright, as if she had never felt the slightest twinge.

Tal didn't say anything. He just threw over the coiled rope. He really didn't understand these Icecarls.

Milla cut through the laces on her claw-hands, removed them, made a loop with the rope and easily flipped it over the top of the pyramid. It seemed secure enough, though she inspected the edges to make sure the crystal would not cut the rope. Once the edges might have been sharp, but long exposure to wind, snow and rain had rounded them off.

Tal caught the end she threw back.

"Tie a pack on," Milla instructed. "And one of the other ropes, so we can lower it down and then back up."

Tal quickly did as he was told. Passing the second rope behind his back, he lowered the pack down till Milla's rope was taut, so she could swing it across and pull it up. They then repeated the process with Tal's pack and one of the lanterns. The other lantern had a rope tied to it, but it would be left till last, so Tal could see where to jump.

Tal was glad that all this delayed his own crossing. He was still trying to work out another way to get across, though there didn't seem to be any alternative. Once again he walked to the edge and looked down. A momentary dizziness hit him and he stepped back suddenly. So suddenly he almost fell.

There had to be another way! Ignoring Milla, he backtracked down the road, holding the lantern up to look at the sheer face of the mountainside. If he could find solid rock, he could climb higher and then across, to get past the gap.

He thought he could see a ledge and for a moment

he was filled with hope. Then he realised it was only an illusion, caused by a band of darker stone.

There was no other way across. No other way if he wanted to get back to the Castle.

Milla threw the rope over again. Tal tied it around himself and then the free end to the specially made loop on his new, wider belt.

"If I don't make it…" he said, then faltered. Even if he asked her to, Milla would never be able to find his father, save his mother, or rescue Gref. And the Chosen did not have posthumous promotions. If he fell here, he would never fulfill his dreams of rising Violet. Brilliance Tal Graile-Rerem, Shadowlord of the Violet Order, would never be…

"What?" shouted Milla.

Tal shook his head slowly, clearing his head of dreams. This time, Milla looped the rope twice more around the pyramid and left only enough slack so that Tal could lay it out to one side of his run, where he wouldn't trip over it.

When everything was ready, Tal backed up into the darkness. He stood there for some time, trying to get his heart to slow down enough so that he could actually tell individual heartbeats apart.

His shadowguard stood next to him, barely visible against the dark stone. It was too weak to be of much use, with only the moth-lanterns for light. Even so, it leaned forward like a racer about to start and Tal knew it was trying to encourage him.

It had got much colder, but Tal wasn't sure how much of that was just from standing still and how much was from fear.

Milla seemed to be a long way away, at the end of a tunnel. A small figure, lit in green, with the pyramid's reflections sparkling around her.

"It's just like the Achievement of the Body," Tal whispered to himself. "Someone has put a Gasping Hole in my way. I win if I jump it. Violet Ray of Attainment. Jump. Win. Jump."

Taking a very deep breath, he started to run. The teeth on his boots shrieked on the stone of the road. Rope whisked up next to him as green light and the darkness of the gap rushed at him, faster and faster.

"Yaaaaaaaahhhhh!" screamed Tal, as he hurled himself forward... into thin air.

The other side of the gap hurtled towards him. He stretched out his arms and pulled up his feet, willing himself further and further on. He knew he wasn't going to make it. In an instant, he would be falling, not jumping, the rope whistling away above his head, his shadowguard weakly scrabbling at handholds—

He hit, fingers reaching for a hold, feet kicking to get the boot-teeth into a foothold. Then he realised he wasn't sliding down a vertical cliff. He was lying flat on the ground, desperately trying to prevent a fall that wasn't going to happen.

He'd made it – and he'd jumped further than Milla!

He lay there, panting, while Milla undid the rope from his belt and the pyramid and coiled it up. She didn't say anything then, or as she stepped over him to bring in the other rope and the lantern.

Eventually Tal got up and picked up his pack. His shadowguard moved into its accustomed place at his feet. Maybe the Icecarls didn't congratulate one another on escaping death. They just got on with it.

Or perhaps not.

"Good jump," Milla said finally, as Tal shrugged his pack into a comfortable position.

"Thanks," Tal replied. But Milla had already pulled her face mask into place and turned away. Walking around the pyramid, she disappeared from sight.

"Look out for the tunnel entrance," Tal said as he hurriedly followed her. "It will be close."

The road continued past the pyramid and was in better shape. Much more of the original metal remained and the mountain had not collapsed on to it. Tal counted out a hundred stretches as he walked, holding his lantern high so he could see anything that might be a tunnel entrance.

But neither of them saw anything. After a hundred and twenty stretches, Milla stopped. She raised her mask and said, "Perhaps the entrance is on the other side."

"What?" asked Tal. He lifted his own mask and looked at Milla. "You mean the other side of the gap! It… it can't be! We would have seen it."

"We *should* have seen it." Milla nodded, her face expressionless. "We will have to jump back."

"No!" exclaimed Tal. "No. It *has* to be on this side."

Milla kept nodding. It took Tal a second to realise that she was trying not to laugh. Then she couldn't hold it in any more and the laughter burst out. Tal couldn't remember even seeing her smile before.

"It is an Icecarl joke!" she spluttered, clapping her fists together. "We always joke about revisiting danger. Like Talgrim One-Arm, who thought he had to go back to kill the Blue Selski when Vilske had already finished it."

"I don't get it," said Tal, shaking his head.

Milla laughed again and pointed.

"Look, we're standing next to the entrance!"

She pointed up above her head. There were square-cut stones laid around a circular hole that led into the mountainside. A tunnel.

Tal stared up at the tunnel in disbelief and felt his crooked smile starting to curve up one side of his face. He could put up with any number of stupid Icecarl jokes to see the way home. Soon he would be back in the Castle. Deliberately, he tried not to think of the troubles that awaited him there.

For now, all they had to do was get in that tunnel and follow the map. How hard could that be?

It was unbearably hot inside the tunnel. Even with a wet cloth over his mouth and nose, Tal could hardly breathe. He was able to take only shallow breaths and the lack of air made him very weak.

Once again he set down his Icecarl moth-lantern to look at the small rectangle of bone he held in his left hand, holding a magnifying glass close to his eyes so he could make out the tiny drawings scratched into the surface.

They had turned left at the last intersection of the narrow, crawl-size tunnels, so at the next intersection they should turn right.

A cough behind him – and then a tap at his heels –

reminded him that Milla must find these overheated tunnels even more unbearable than he did. She was an Icecarl, born to travel the frozen wastelands. Tal had at least experienced real heat before, though this tunnel was even hotter than the Orchard Gardens or his sick mother's sunchamber.

He started crawling forwards again. His shadowguard flowed ahead of him, avoiding Milla. It was stronger in the confined space of the tunnels, where the light reflected from the walls, and so more noticeable.

At the next intersection, Tal looked at the miniature map once more. According to the carving they should turn right. But the boy hesitated. The light from the moth-lantern was green and illuminated only a small area. Up ahead, in the right-hand tunnel, there was a faint red glow.

Tal was afraid he knew what that meant. He and Milla were in a network of tunnels that had probably once been used by the builders of the Castle's heating system. Below them – he hoped far below – there were much larger tunnels that channelled lava from the depths of the mountain.

These tunnels heated vast reservoirs of water, the steam from which was then piped up to heat the Castle's many levels and rooms.

The red glow ahead suggested that one of the lava tunnels had broken open and its deadly contents had bubbled their way up. The bone map in Tal's hand was very old and any number of changes could have taken place since it was made.

To make matters worse, the map didn't show any other way of getting into the Castle. In fact, apart from showing the key intersections, it had no detail at all. So Tal *couldn't* work out another way to go.

He took another shallow breath and started forwards again. He could hear Milla following him, shuffling along in a half crouch, half crawl. She was coughing a lot, but hadn't said anything. She probably wouldn't, even if she was about to pass out. From what Tal had seen, a Shield Maiden would probably keep on crawling even if she *had* passed out...

The red light grew stronger and became tinged with an even brighter yellow. It got hotter too, the stone of the tunnel almost too warm to touch with bare skin. For the first time, Tal regretted dumping their heavy outer coats back near the beginning of the tunnels, though Milla still wore her Selski-hide armour. She probably never took it off, Tal thought, like the Merwin-horn sword glowing at her side.

At the next intersection, Tal had to wipe the sweat off his forehead and out of his eyes before he could focus on the bone map. Another right turn, and this time the red light came from all directions. There had to be a lot of lava ahead.

The air smelled even worse than it had before. Tal lay on his side to rewet his breathing rag from the water bottle the Shield Maidens had given him, a hollowed-out Wreska bone with a hide stopper. Milla did the same, then put her bone mask back on over the top. Tal had long since removed his, but Milla treated the mask like armour, to be worn at all times. Tal caught a brief glimpse of her pale face, set in determination, before the mask and its amber lenses hid her expression.

"Not much further," croaked Tal.

Milla shrugged and answered, "I know you can't help crawling slowly."

"That's not... oh, never mind!" snapped Tal. Why had he bothered to waste his breath?

It took a long time to reach the next intersection. Not because it was a long way, but because they were both so sapped of energy by the heat and the lack of air.

Tal was so busy concentrating on keeping the lantern up and keeping himself moving forwards that he forgot to look ahead. He actually ran into the skeleton before he realised what was going on.

When Tal *did* look to see what he'd bumped into, he backed up so quickly that he smacked into Milla. She cried out angrily and for a moment there was a tangle of his legs and her arms before Tal calmed down and Milla moved back.

"What... is... it?" she said, speaking with effort, taking a breath between each word.

"A skeleton," puffed Tal. He twisted the knob on the lamp to open the weave, letting more light from the luminous moths shine out. Tal's shadowguard slid back under his feet as he did so, to fall behind like a real shadow. Milla shuffled back still further, so the shadowguard couldn't touch her.

The skeleton had obviously been there a long time, or else it had been scoured clean by scavengers. There were no scraps of clothing, or anything that might be a clue to who it was. Probably not an Icecarl, Tal thought, because there were no signs of any weapon. He'd never seen an unarmed Icecarl.

They would have to climb over the skeleton to get past. Steeling himself, Tal closed his eyes and reached out, but as his fingers touched bone he pulled them back. He couldn't help imagining that it was still someone's arm, and the skeleton would sit up and shout.

"Let me do it!" ordered Milla, but Tal wouldn't get out of her way.

He reached out and tugged at one arm, to pull the whole skeleton flat so they could crawl over it. But as he tugged, the arm came off, and then every individual bone fell apart. Tal gasped and dropped the arm. Something else fell too, and clinked on the stone.

Tal saw it fall between his feet and roll behind him. A finger bone, with a ring stuck on it. A ring with a large jewel.

A Sunstone!

Tal pushed his back against the tunnel wall, ignoring the heat of the rock, and looked behind. Milla was picking up the finger bone and sliding off the ring. As she touched it, the jewel suddenly blossomed into light, swinging wildly through every colour in the spectrum. It was so bright that Tal had to close his eyes.

When he opened them again, Milla had closed her hand around the Sunstone ring. Light leaked out between her fingers and made her hand translucent.

"Give... it... to... me," said Tal. It was what he needed, what he had climbed the Red Tower to get – a new, powerful Sunstone, which he could use to become a full Chosen, to enter the spirit world of Aenir and save his family.

"No." Milla started to turn around.

"Wait!" Tal croaked. He twisted around, but Milla was quicker. She had already gone several stretches along the tunnel. "You don't know how to use it! And you'll... get... lost!"

Milla kept going. She probably remembered the turns, Tal thought. But he had to have the Sunstone. He could always get her another one later. He looked down at his shadowguard. Milla would never forgive him if he used it... but if he didn't...

"Shadowguard, shadowguard," coughed Tal. "Grab that girl, as quick as you can."

The shadowguard shot out from under him, growing long and thin, like the shadow of a slender giant. One arm grew even longer, and the hand on the end spread wide. It snatched at Milla's ankle and gripped tight.

Instantly, she rolled on her back, flexed forward and struck at the shadow with a bone knife that sprung out of her sleeve. But that couldn't hurt the shadowguard and it held fast.

"Traitor!" hissed Milla. "You swore!"

Tal *had* sworn with his own blood and Milla's to get a Sunstone for the Far Raiders. He had the triple scar on his wrist to prove it. But he hadn't sworn to hand over the *first* Sunstone they came across.

"You swore too," he said. "To help me reach the Castle. We aren't really there yet. Besides, that Sunstone isn't tuned."

Milla hesitated, but only for a second. She thought they were close enough to the Castle. Then she started crawling again, dragging the shadowguard with her.

"I saved your life!" Tal panted out desperately when Milla didn't stop. The shadowguard wasn't strong enough to hold Milla for long and he didn't want to tell it to hurt her. "You owe me."

Milla stopped as if she had run into a wall. Tal had saved her life when his shadowguard had bound her wounds after the fight with the one-eyed Merwin. Arguably, she had saved his by killing the Merwin, but that was not so certain.

"I need that Sunstone," coughed Tal. "Come with me and I'll get you another one. If I can't within fourteen sleeps... I'll give it back. For the ship and... the clan."

Milla's knife disappeared up her sleeve. Then she opened her hand. Tal had to shield his eyes from the Sunstone's light as she threw the ring back to him.

"Fourteen sleeps!" Milla conceded angrily. "But I no longer owe you a life!"

"Agreed," said Tal. He picked up the ring and focused his mind on the Sunstone. It flared up again, then gradually dimmed as Tal took control. When it was no brighter than the moth-lantern, Tal tried the ring on his middle finger. It was too big, so he fastened it to the chain around his neck, next to the chunk of blackened rock that had been his old Sunstone.

The Sunstone in the ring was very old, but it had lost none of its power, lying unused here in the dark. The Chosen – for the skeleton must have been a Chosen – had made it go dormant before he or she died. That surprised Tal. He knew no Chosen of his time brave enough to die alone in the dark, just to save a Sunstone.

"Shadowguard, shadowguard," he muttered. "Come back to me."

The shadowguard let go of Milla and hastily retreated, flowing back into a regular shadow. One arm kept moving, waving backward and forward.

"What?" Tal asked. His mind felt a bit fuzzy.

The shadowguard waved again and Tal realised it was telling him to hurry. At the same time, he became aware that Milla had caught up to him again and he hadn't even noticed. He must have blanked out for a few seconds.

"Air," Milla gasped. "Bad air."

She pushed at him. Tal turned and started crawling again.

They crawled for what seemed like hours but couldn't have been more than minutes. Then they were at yet another intersection. Slowly, Tal got out the bone map and tried to work out where they were. The red glow was bright, but not bright enough to read by, and for some reason the moth-lantern had dimmed. Tal shook it to liven up the moths, but that didn't work and the spaces in the weave were as wide as they could go.

It was hard work to set the lamp down and get the new Sunstone out instead, since Tal's hands seemed to be weighed down and wouldn't go where he told them to. He finally managed it, and after a few bright flashes he did get the Sunstone to shine at a useful level.

In its light, he saw that all the luminous moths in the lantern were lying still on the bottom, their green abdomens fading. The moths were asleep... or dead. Sluggishly, Tal passed the lantern back to Milla. It was an Icecarl tool. She would know what to do with it.

He looked back at the map. It took some time to remember where they were. A right turn, and then a symbol that might represent a ladder, or perhaps a ramp. A way up, anyway.

Tal hoped.

Unless they were only at the intersection before that, in which case they should take a left and then a right. But they'd already done that, hadn't they?

Tal turned the map the other way up. Now that he looked at it, he wasn't sure that he hadn't had it upside down the whole time.

"On!" whispered Milla."We must… go on!"

Tal couldn't remember which way they had turned, but after a while they came to an opening in the tunnel ceiling and a ladder of the same crystal as the Crystal Wood in the Castle. Tal tried to direct a beam of light at it to make it sing, but for some reason he kept missing. Different-coloured beams shot out everywhere from the Sunstone, but none hit.

It made Tal laugh. He couldn't help it – a choking giggle came out of him that sounded so strange, he looked around to see whom it might belong to.

Dimly he was aware of Milla pushing past him and starting to climb, then of his shadowguard pulling at him, placing his hands on the ladder and his foot on the lowest rung.

The ladder was strangely cool, here where everything was hot. The shock of it cleared Tal's head a little and he realised with sudden panic that there was something poisonous in the air, fumes from the lava down below, that made his head strange and his limbs full of lead.

The shadowguard pulled at Tal's wrist, urging

him to climb. Milla was only just ahead of him, climbing very slowly. She almost slipped a few times, but the shadowguard was watching her too, and it zipped past to put her feet or hands back on the ladder.

Tal started seeing double. He reached for rungs that weren't there and his fingers closed on air instead of crystal. His arms grew too tired to reach up. Slowly, ever so slowly, he put his legs through the ladder and sat, fumbling with his belt. He couldn't go on, but he could try and strap himself to the ladder so he wouldn't fall.

He managed to get his belt around the ladder. Then a final cautious thought made him slip the chain with the Sunstone over his head. For an instant it seemed certain he would drop it, before his shadowguard helped his trembling hand push it into the secret pocket inside his sleeve.

Then he passed out, only his broad Selski-hide belt looped through the ladder preventing him from falling.

Milla lasted a little longer. She made it to a landing thirty stretches above, but that was all.

Collapsing on to it, she only just managed to draw her knife – to face death armed – before she passed out as well.

The shadowguard made sure Tal's belt was secure, then tried to climb further up the ladder. But as it passed the landing where Milla lay, it grew thinner and more transparent. A few stretches further, it was no more than a dark outline, without substance. Reluctantly, it drew back, till it once again seemed like Tal's natural shadow.

Nothing could help Tal now.

"Kill them."

Tal heard the words as if they came from a long way off, carried on the wind. Somewhere, someone was talking about killing someone. Someone else was saying, "No. We don't know who they are."

"One looks like a Chosen. I say kill *him* at least."

"What's the point of dragging them up here, if we just kill them anyway? They haven't got Sunstones, they've both got normal shadows and look at their clothes. They must be from somewhere else. Maybe they can help us."

The one who wanted to kill whoever it was laughed – a bitter, mocking laugh.

"Help us do what? Hide in these tunnels better? Live more miserably than we do now?"

Tal managed to get one eye open a fraction and saw that the people talking were standing quite close to him. There were three of them. Two boys who couldn't be much older than he was, and another taller one who looked a bit older. He hadn't spoken.

The two younger ones carried short, broad-bladed spears. They were all wearing dirty rags that Tal thought might once have been white Underfolk robes. The older one had a cap with a long black feather in it.

There was an oil lamp sitting on the floor behind the three boys. Its light cast long shadows from all three. Natural shadows.

They *were* Underfolk. Tal tried to order them to help him, but nothing came out. The effort needed to keep even one eyelid half open was immense.

"Kill them," said the first, blond boy.

"Talk to them," said the second boy.

Who were they talking about? Tal wanted to turn his head to see, but his neck wouldn't move, either. Maybe it was all a dream.

Both turned to the boy with the feather in his cap. Obviously he had to make the decision.

"Neither. We take them up to the top of the service levels and leave them there. They'll come round in an hour or so."

"Oh, Crow," complained the blond boy. "What'll that do?"

So the older boy with the feather was called Crow, thought Tal muzzily. The black feather had to be from a crow then. But the only crows in the Castle were pets of very high Chosen. There was an old legend that when the last crow left the Castle, it would mean the end of the Chosen and the seven Towers would fall.

"Unless I'm wrong, taking them up will deliver a problem to the Chosen," said Crow. "Gill, go and get Clovil and Ferek. We'll have to carry them."

Tal watched Gill, the second speaker, walk out of his field of vision. Gill was a girl's name, which was odd. Unless Gill *was* a girl. She might be, Tal thought, watching her disappear. His one half-open eye closed and could not be reopened.

Things got even more dreamlike then. He felt

himself floating up from the floor as weird noises echoed all around him. Possibly they were meant to be words, but Tal couldn't get a grip on them. They kept changing shape and slipping away. Words that some unconscious part of his brain knew were "up" and "heavy" and "you carry him then" became "snurp" and "preefy" and "loll garly slimwen."

Nothing made sense. It was too hard. Tal fell back into total unconsciousness.

When he awoke the second time, he had a moment's perfect recall of his first waking. Then it was gone, replaced by a blinding headache that stabbed him right between the eyes.

He groaned and sat up, cradling his head in his hands. Then he remembered that he was tied to a ladder in the heating tunnels.

Tal snatched his hands away from his eyes and looked around.

He wasn't hanging off a ladder. He was lying on the floor of a hallway lit by a small Sunstone in the ceiling. There was another Sunstone about ten stretches on, and another ten stretches beyond that. They were plain white Sunstones of very little power.

Something made a noise. Tal whipped round, and wished he hadn't as his headache struck even more savagely.

The noise was from Milla. She was sitting cross-legged behind him, slowly breathing in and out with great control. She had taken off her face mask and her skin had a nasty greenish tinge.

Tal pressed his thumbs into his temples and muttered, "What happened?"

Milla let out her breath very, very slowly.

"Bad air. Some people found us and carried us here. There was some talk of killing, but they didn't really want to. Lucky your shadow behaved itself. I think they would have killed you if it hadn't."

"Oh," said Tal, a vague memory coming back. "I thought that was a dream. Were you awake then?"

Milla looked embarrassed. She started to take in a breath as if to ignore the question, then let it out suddenly and said, "I only recovered enough to hear. I couldn't move. You should take deep, slow breaths. It will clear the bad air out of your blood."

Tal nodded, but didn't change his breathing.

Those people had to be renegade Underfolk. And they'd talked about his Sunstone!

His hand flew to his neck. The chain with the old and the new Sunstone wasn't there! He had a moment of panic, before his shadowguard plucked at his sleeve, reminding him that the chain was in the secret pocket. He pulled it out and dropped it over his head with a sigh of relief.

"Thirteen sleeps, then it's mine," Milla said, watching him check the Sunstone. "We've just had one sleep."

Tal scowled at her. Slowly, he got up and walked a little way along the corridor. Every step sent stabs of pain through his head.

"Are we in your Castle now?" asked Milla. She pointed at the ceiling. "There are many Sunstones. Perhaps I should dig one out."

"They're too small," said Tal wearily. "They only last a few months before they have to be replaced. You can't do anything with them either. They just give light."

Milla shrugged. "Light is a lot, in the dark."

Tal sighed. From the low level of light and the

whitewashed walls of the corridor, they seemed to be on one of the Underfolk levels. There were lots of Underfolk levels, where the servants lived and worked and farmed. But Tal didn't think of these levels as part of the *real* Castle.

When they left these levels, they would be entering the Castle proper. Tal was suddenly struck by the realisation that he had actually got back. He'd never thought beyond that, and now he didn't know what to do. What *could* he do?

He couldn't just go home, because his enemies would find him. He couldn't go to any public places dressed the way he was. There'd be a panic, or a lot of trouble at the least.

And that was just Tal. He hadn't properly thought about bringing Milla into the Castle at all. He knew she was an Icecarl and what that meant. No one else would. There was no knowing how the Chosen would react. As far as they were concerned no one lived outside the Castle. No one *could* live outside the Castle. They would think she was some kind of creature that had crossed from Aenir without becoming a shadow. A free spirit. An uncontrolled spirit.

That would be about the most frightening thing a Chosen could imagine. There would be white-hot rays of light and destruction, with Chosen blasting them on first sight. That's what Tal would have done if he'd encountered Milla in the Castle, he knew. If she wasn't a Chosen and wasn't an Underfolk, she had to be a monster. Why would any other Chosen think differently?

"Are we in your Castle now?" asked Milla again. She looked around at the bare, smooth walls. There were no trophies, no horned Merwin skulls or Selski flipper-toe bones, or the captured weapons of enemies. "It's not very impressive. Your guards should have found us by now, instead of those Outcasts."

"Those what?" asked Tal. He hadn't been listening. He was consumed by a new fear. What if he had done the absolutely wrong thing in bringing Milla to the Castle?

"Outcasts," said Milla. "That's what the people who brought us here were, weren't they? People without a clan, who follow the ship and live on scraps and scrapings?"

Tal stared at Milla. He'd never seen her so talkative before. Maybe it was something to do with the bad air. Or perhaps she was simply relieved they'd made it through the searing heat of the tunnels.

"I don't know who they were," he replied. "Underfolk. Servants. But I think ones who have escaped. They must live somewhere down here."

"Servants who cannot choose to leave?" asked Milla as she got up and flexed her arms. "You mean thralls. Some clans have them, though the Crones do not like it. The Far Raiders will not trade with thrall-takers."

"What's a thrall?" asked Tal. He hadn't heard the word before.

"Servants who cannot leave," said Milla. Seeing that Tal still didn't understand, she added, "People who can be bought and sold."

"Oh," said Tal. "Well, the Underfolk are different. Most of them are born to be servants... or they ended up as Underfolk for... good reasons. And they don't get bought and sold. Just reassigned."

"A thrall by any other name still stinks the ship," said Milla.

She emphasised this with a shrug and did two cartwheels along the corridor, to loosen up her muscles. Tal groaned and hit his head even more forcefully. Out of the corner of his eye he saw his shadowguard copy his action, until Milla noticed. Then it slid back to become a natural shadow once more.

Tal watched it go. It was only then he realised that he wasn't as pleased to be back as he should be. He should be kissing the floor and laughing with joy. After all, he'd survived a fall of thousands of stretches from the Red Tower. He'd lived through an encounter with Icecarls. He'd crossed the Living Sea. He'd helped kill a Merwin. He'd seen the Ruin Ship, climbed the Mountain of Light and made it through the heatway tunnels.

But he didn't feel joyful. He felt tired, as if all this was only the beginning. He'd always thought that he'd go straight to his family's rooms when he returned, and see his mother. But that wasn't possible.

The trouble was, he didn't know what to do instead.

Milla cartwheeled back, reminding him that he'd

brought the particular problem she represented on himself.

"What now?" asked Milla. "Do we go and meet your clan Crone?"

"Um," said Tal, brightening as an idea suddenly came to him. "Not exactly – but close to it!"

"We're going to see a wise man," explained Tal, as they crept along the corridor that led to a stair up to the first Red level. "My great-uncle Ebbitt. He will help us work out what to do next."

And, Tal thought, he'll know what to do about Milla. Perhaps she could hide out while Tal found her a Sunstone.

Milla nodded, silent once again. Tal noted that her hand was on her sword and her eyes constantly in movement, searching for enemies.

"He has a Spiritshadow," Tal added. "All the Chosen do. But they won't do anything unless they are ordered to."

"These Spiritshadows are like your little shadow, but bigger?" asked Milla.

"They're not always bigger," said Tal. "But stronger and more dangerous. They can't change shape like a shadowguard, but they can stretch and twist the shape they've got."

Milla thought about this for a while. A few steps further on she asked, "What happens to a Spiritshadow when its master is killed?"

Tal shook his head.

"The Spiritshadow fades with them—"

He broke off, reminded of his mother. She *had* to still be alive.

"Perhaps we will find out," said Milla.

Tal stopped and turned to look Milla in the eye.

"Milla, you can't fight in the Castle!" he warned her. "We have to be careful as it is. No one has ever come in from outside before. If you attack someone, it will just make everything worse."

"I only fight if I am attacked," said Milla. "But you are afraid of something. Why should you be afraid in your own ship... your own home?"

"I'm not afraid!" Tal snapped. "It's complicated.

There are some Chosen who don't like my family, and there are some other things happening that I don't understand. I'm just being cautious."

"You know very little," said Milla. "I do not think your Chosen teach their children well. We would not let anyone off the ship who was so ignorant of the Ice."

Tal started to reply, but he was too furious to get any words out. He took a long, slow breath and finally managed to say, "It is *very* complicated, because it has to do with people, not animals or, or... the weather! *You* don't have the education to understand. So just follow me and be quiet!"

"I know how to be quiet," agreed Milla. "I can be much quieter than you."

"Good," snapped Tal. "Start now!"

They didn't meet anyone on the stairs or in the corridor that led to Ebbitt's rather strange quarters. This was not surprising, since Ebbitt had chosen to live in the least-used part of the lowest Red level. Apart from him, everyone here was a Dimmer – the lowest possible rank in Chosen society – and was desperate to rise.

As they left the stairs, Milla noticed the faint

red tinge to the Sunstones in the corridor and the faded red stripes that adorned the ceiling, and asked about them. Tal found himself giving a garbled explanation about the different Orders and levels, which Milla reduced down to the rather simplistic "Many clans live in your Castle."

This whispered conversation lasted until they came to the beginning of the corridor that Ebbitt used as one big room. As usual, the entrance was blocked with a jumble of furniture and odds and ends. Strangely, there was no sign of the wardrobe that Tal had used before as a gate. In fact, there was no obvious way to get through the tangle of upended tables, stacked chairs, spiked hat stands, cabinets, carpets, marble sculptures and wallhangings.

"Great-uncle Ebbitt is a bit…" Tal said, eyeing the pile that reached nearly to the ceiling. "Well, he's not exactly normal."

Milla nodded, then suddenly stepped back, her hand on the hilt of her Merwin-horn sword.

Tal couldn't see what Milla had reacted to, until she pointed to a large blue cushion at the base of the piled furniture. It was slowly moving outward, almost without a sound. Then it fell over, revealing a narrow triangular gap where two chairs had been leaning back-to-back. "Why couldn't you just have a door?" Tal asked, addressing the narrow tunnel through the furniture barrier. He got down on his knees and peered in. There was no sign of Ebbitt, but the falling cushion was clearly the old man's idea of a welcome.

"Come on," Tal said to Milla, stretching out so he could slide through the gap. "It might look like it's going to fall down, but Ebbitt's an expert at this sort of thing."

"There is wisdom behind all this rubbish?" asked Milla, but she knelt down, ready to follow Tal.

The barrier of piled-up bits and pieces went much further than Tal had expected. He had to wriggle through several turns before he finally emerged into a relatively clear area. Once again, everything had changed. There was no sign of Ebbitt's faded throne. But Ebbitt was there, dressed in an Underfolk robe of white and a jacket in the Indigo colour forbidden to him since his decline to the Red.

He was lying on a long, heavily cushioned lounge, with a sleep blindfold wrapped around his eyes. His Spiritshadow, a great maned cat, was sitting at his feet, watching Tal emerge.

"Go away," said Ebbitt, waving a languid hand. "I have a headache."

"So do I," Tal replied. "I need your help, Uncle Ebbitt. It's very important."

"So important that you haven't been to see me in two weeks?" Ebbitt asked, without moving.

"I don't believe this!" Tal shouted. "I haven't been to see you because I FELL OFF THE RED TOWER!"

His shout made Ebbitt wince, but it had a more dramatic effect on Ebbitt's Spiritshadow. It leaped to its feet and stood poised to spring.

Then Tal realised it wasn't his shout the Spiritshadow was reacting to. Milla had just climbed out of the gap in the barrier.

"Don't do anything!" Tal ordered, though he wasn't sure whether he was talking to Milla or the Spiritshadow.

"What is going on?" Ebbitt asked testily. He tore off his blindfold and sat up, blinking. When he saw Milla, who had drawn her sword despite Tal's instruction, he raised his hand, the Sunstone ring on his finger swirling with sudden light.

"Don't!" Tal exclaimed again. "Don't anyone do anything."

"Who... or what... is that?" asked Ebbitt as he slowly got to his feet. He didn't lower his hand.

Tal saw that Milla had put her face mask back on and her hood up. The amber lenses shone horribly in the Sunstone light, and the mouth-hole was horribly dark. She *did* look like a monster.

"Please take off your mask, Milla," he sighed. "No one is going to attack you, right, Uncle?"

"If you say so," said Ebbitt, who seemed slightly relieved to hear the word *mask*, and even more so when Milla slowly removed it. "But again I ask, who are you? You have a natural shadow, but you do not look like any Underfolk I have ever seen."

"I am Milla of the Far Raiders. Daughter of Ylse, daughter of Emor, daughter of Rohen, daughter of Clyo, in the line of Danir since the Ruin of the Ship."

Ebbitt sat back down.

"She's from outside," said Tal. "They call themselves Icecarls."

Ebbitt didn't say anything. His Spiritshadow

turned to look at him, then lumbered over to touch his face with one shadowy paw.

"Uncle Ebbitt?" Tal said, suddenly anxious.

The Spiritshadow pushed hard at Ebbitt's chest and the old man let out a sudden, wheezing cough.

"Outside?" he gasped. "Outside the Castle?"

"Yes," Tal explained. "That's where I've been. I really did fall off the Red Tower. My shadowguard saved me."

Ebbitt took a deep breath, then reached under the lounge to pull out a long crystal bottle with a narrow neck. Tal saw that there was a glass next to it, but Ebbitt didn't bother with that. He pulled out the stopper and took several long drinks.

"Distilled cordial of Halo-flower," he said, setting it down. "From Aenir. Medicine for a mad old man. Come closer, Milla, daughter of Ylse and... all those others."

"You can put your sword away too," Tal said, then added in an aside to Ebbitt, "It's made from a Merwin horn. That's why it glows."

Milla hesitated, then sheathed her sword and approached. A few feet away, she clapped her fists together, in the Icecarl salute.

"So there is some truth to the old legends," said Ebbitt, peering at Milla in fascination. "There is more out there than ice and snow."

"Much more," said Tal, with considerable feeling. "Most of it trying to kill me."

"Tell me everything," Ebbitt exclaimed, flapping his arms up and down in excitement. "This is the best thing that's happened in years."

"What about Mother?" asked Tal. "How is she? And Gref? And Kusi? What's happened while I've been gone?"

"Your mother is still not well," said Ebbitt evasively. He got up and went to a cupboard, fetching food and a bottle of sweetwater, obviously more suitable for his current guests than the distillation of Halo-flowers. "We will talk about them later. First, I must hear your story."

Tal frowned, but from long experience he knew he couldn't make Ebbitt do anything he didn't want to do. The quickest way to find out anything from his great-uncle would be to tell him what had happened.

"After I left you," he started, "I climbed the Red Tower..."

Ebbitt paced up and down as Tal spoke. Occasionally he interrupted to ask questions, mostly of Tal, but also of Milla. Sometimes he laughed and sometimes he clapped his hands together and his laugh became a cackle. Milla moved back a bit when he did this, and her eyes flicked between the old man and the Spiritshadow.

She knew that Ebbitt must be as old as the Crone Mother of the Far Raiders, but he didn't look it. His hair was silver, not white, and grew long at the back while it receded at the front. His skin was lined, but his wrinkles could not compete with any Crone Mother's.

He was much taller than she'd expected and moved more briskly. But his most dominant feature was his nose. In an Icecarl saga, Ebbitt would definitely be called Ebbitt Greatnose.

"Now," said Tal, as he finished with their strange rescue from the heating tunnels. "What about Gref? And Kusi? And Mother?"

"Your brother, Gref, is missing," Ebbitt said heavily. "I thought he might be with you and that you were merely lying low to avoid the bloated Sushin. Kusi is with those tainted products of my niece's marriage, I'm afraid."

*The bloated Sushin* was Tal's enemy, Shadowmaster Sushin. It took Tal a second to realise that *the tainted products of my niece's marriage* meant his mother's cousins, Lallek and Korrek. They were just as bad as Sushin. Worse really, since they were supposed to be family. His small sister would not like being with them.

"But we wouldn't have tried to hide without telling Mother." Tal frowned. "You should've asked her! Anything could have happened to Gref!"

"I'm afraid I have not been able to speak to Graile,"

Ebbitt replied carefully. "She fell into a very deep sleep the day you disappeared – and has not awoken."

"What!" exclaimed Tal. His fingers twitched as he paced the room. "She wasn't that bad when I left. I should have—"

"There is nothing you could have done," said Ebbitt. "She sleeps to save her strength. I think she can be awakened, but only as a last resort. It should not be done until she can be taken into Aenir on the Day of Ascension. There are several magics to be found there that will heal her spirit and thus her flesh."

"I can take her into Aenir," exclaimed Tal, pulling out his new Sunstone. "I could do it today. I don't care about waiting for the Day."

Milla stirred, her hand once more falling to her sword. Tal looked at her, and slowly shook his head.

"No, I guess I can't," he said, letting the Sunstone fall back under his fur coat. "If you're sure Mother will just sleep till the Day of Ascension, then I should... well, Kusi will be miserable, but at least she's safe. So I need to find Gref, and get a Sunstone for Milla."

Ebbitt looked at the Icecarl girl.

"I don't think most of the Chosen are ready to hear about Icecarls and their ships and the Ice," he said. "You will have to disguise yourself as an Underfolk, Milla."

"Shield Maidens do not hide behind false banners," said Milla proudly. It sounded like she was reciting a rule.

"Mmmm," replied Ebbitt. "Perhaps we can discuss that later. As to finding Gref, I do have one small idea. One very small idea. So small that it could disappear if I don't snatch hold of it—"

"What idea, Uncle?" Tal interrupted. Ebbitt was starting to hop round in a circle, as if his idea were something he could physically pursue.

"Ssshhh," said Ebbitt. "I've almost got it!"

He made a sudden snatch and clapped his hands around seemingly thin air.

"Have you got it?" Tal asked. "The idea?"

Ebbitt opened his palms and inspected something.

"What?" he asked. "No, it's a piece of fluff. I wonder where that came from?"

Tal glanced at Milla. She was expressionless as

usual, but a muscle under her eye twitched, just for a second. He hoped it was amusement.

"What about the idea?" he asked. "To find Gref."

Ebbitt blew the invisible piece of fluff off his palm.

"The Spiritshadow who took Gref away, outside the Red Tower," he said. He seemed to be addressing the air in front of him, rather than Tal. "You saw it clearly and remember what it looked like?"

"Yes," said Tal. He moved round so he was in front of Ebbitt, but the old man swivelled on one foot so he was looking at the wall. "It had the shape of a Borzog. I recognised it from your Beastmaker game."

"An unusual Spiritshadow," said Ebbitt. "Not one I have seen before. I know one thing though."

"What?" asked Tal in exasperation, after Ebbitt didn't continue.

"Or two things actually," said Ebbitt, counting on his fingers. "One, two."

"What!"

"One. You must identify who that Spiritshadow's master is." Ebbitt folded back his finger so hard that he flinched. "Ow!"

"And the second thing?" Tal prompted.

"Second. The only reliable way to do this is to look that Spiritshadow up in the Codex."

"The Codex?"

"The Codex of All Things," Ebbitt whispered. "The Compendium of the Chosen. The record of our race, inscribed in light upon crystal. Speak and it shall answer. The greatest magic ever to come out of Aenir. The Codex that knows all names – all Chosen, all Spiritshadows, all shadowguards."

"Well, finding out who the Borzog Spiritshadow answers to will be a start," said Tal, though he was a little worried by the gleam in his great-uncle's eye. "Where can I find this Codex?"

"That's the catch," Ebbitt said dolefully. He collapsed back into his lounge. "It disappeared more than twenty years ago. Lost, to our great sorrow. Or stolen, which I am beginning to think might be the case. If that is true, then it is for reasons so horrible that I have forced myself to forget them."

Tal groaned and collapsed next to his great-uncle. His shadowguard crept to his feet and turned into a Dattu again, all floppy-eared and harmless.

Ebbitt's Spiritshadow leaned across and licked it, a great shadow-tongue suddenly appearing from its dark mouth. Tal had never seen it do anything like that before and was momentarily shocked.

"Why—" he began to say, when shadowguard, Spiritshadow and Milla all suddenly stiffened to attention, heads turning to the furniture barrier and the entrance to the corridor.

Tal looked too. To his horror, he saw dark shadows sliding under the mass of chairs and bric-a-brac. Long shadows, with a shape he recognised – almost manlike creatures, but with very broad shoulders and impossibly thin waists.

The Spiritshadows of the Imperial Guard! Once Tal would not have been afraid of them, but now he knew some of the guard were in league with Sushin. How had they known he was back already?

"Out!" shouted Ebbitt. "This way!"

Ebbitt was up and over the back of the couch before Tal even realised what was happening. Ebbitt's great maned Spiritshadow was gone a moment later.

Tal hesitated. Should he run from the Imperial

Guard? If they were true guards, they might take him before the Empress and he would get the chance to set everything straight. But if they were Sushin's cronies—

One of the Spiritshadows lunged forward and a cold, shimmering hand clutched him around the ankle. Tal's own shadowguard jumped to his defence, but was instantly batted away.

The Spiritshadow pulled and Tal went down. Too late, he tried to get his Sunstone out. He almost had it free when the Spiritshadow flowed across him, horribly swift, pinning him to the floor.

The hard landing on the floor and the cold, unpleasant touch of the Spiritshadow made up Tal's mind.

"Run, Milla!" he shouted. "Follow Ebbitt!"

Milla jumped to the top of a cupboard, but not to get away. A Spiritshadow stretched itself up to attack her, but before it could, she stabbed it with her Merwin-horn sword.

Usually, physical objects could not hurt a Spiritshadow, so Tal was amazed to see the luminous sword actually tear through the Spiritshadow's head as if it were paper; ribbons of shadow flying out from the blade's passage.

The Spiritshadow shrieked, a noise Tal had never heard before. Then it hastily drew back, out of reach of the sword.

"Ha!" shouted Milla. "Death to shadows!"

She jumped across to another wardrobe and slashed at the third Spiritshadow. It withdrew too, stepping back as the sword left a trail of light through the air.

Light – that was why the sword worked on the Spiritshadows. They could only be harmed by light, and Milla's sword had the right colour and intensity, even in its faded state.

Not that this helped Tal. The Spiritshadow on top of him did not let go and Milla couldn't come down without exposing herself to a simultaneous attack from all three Spiritshadows.

"No!" shouted Tal. He was suddenly afraid, afraid of the Spiritshadow that held him and of what the others would do to Milla, more afraid than he had ever been, even out on the Ice. It was like being attacked by the lectors who had taught him since childhood, a sudden craziness that he couldn't understand and couldn't predict. "Don't fight! Run!"

His shout was still echoing when Milla jumped down, struck at the back of the Spiritshadow that held him, snapped into a roll on the floor and came out of the roll to spin on one foot. Her sword whistled in a complete circle around her – cutting right through the tiny waists of the other two Spiritshadows.

Tal crawled free as his Spiritshadow attacker let go. Somehow he got to his feet and saw that two of the Spiritshadows had literally been cut in half. Unfortunately, each half still seemed to work and they were now coming at Milla. The other Spiritshadow was still, its shadow-flesh slowly rippling back together where it had been cleaved apart.

Tal pulled out his Sunstone and started to concentrate on it.

He was about to unleash a bolt of pure light at the Spiritshadows when the whole furniture barrier exploded behind him in a burst of blinding fire.

# 12

Most of the furniture disappeared in the flash, followed a moment later by a rolling cloud of smoke and hot ash. A rush of Chosen in the uniforms of the Imperial Guard stormed in – with even more Spiritshadows.

Tal had been knocked down by the blast and was momentarily stunned. He couldn't believe they'd blasted the whole corridor. For all they knew there could have been lots of Chosen here, not just himself and Ebbitt.

Dazed by the shock, he staggered to his feet and was sweeping hot ashes off his cheek when he was knocked down a third time, by one of the guards.

The guard immediately knelt on Tal's back and twisted his arms up so he couldn't get at his Sunstone or a weapon.

"Got him!" yelled the guard.

"You get down from there!" another guard shouted at Milla. He didn't sound too concerned, which puzzled Tal. Then he realised that they must have thought she was an Underfolk renegade and that *Tal* was the one who had damaged the Spiritshadows.

Underestimating Milla was not something anyone did more than once, Tal thought. But this time she needed to run, not fight. Desperately he willed her to run. His mouth seemed to be full of ash so he couldn't shout.

Milla didn't run. Tal heard a cry of surprised pain from the guard who'd ordered her down. He craned his head back to see, but all he caught was a pair of boots staggering back, many other boots charging forward and lots of Spiritshadows moving around.

"It's not an Underfolk!"

"Some sort of creature, use Light!"

"Ware the sword!"

"Stand back!"

There was another flash of light and another explosion of ashes. But it hadn't hit Milla. A Spiritshadow screeched, followed by cursing and shouting from the guards and the strange belling sound of steel meeting Merwin horn.

"Watch out! Left, go left!"

"Stay clear, stay – aarrghh!"

"Harl! Japen! That way. Ranil, drag that one back!"

Ranil let go of Tal's arms and started dragging him back by the ankles. From the shouting and running that was going on all around him, it was clear Milla was still free. But there were too many guards and Spiritshadows for her to resist for long.

"Milla!" Tal shouted again, spitting out ash. "Get away! They'll kill you!"

As he yelled, Tal writhed about, and momentarily broke free. Ranil cursed and tried to grab him again, while Tal kicked and wriggled and rolled around on the ground. He got under a table, but there was nowhere to go from there.

In the few seconds he was hidden from view, Tal pulled the Sunstone ring off the chain and hid it in his mouth. He kept the chain in his hand, with the old burnt-out Sunstone still on it.

Ranil ripped the table away and sat on him again, but Tal was at an angle where he could see more of the corridor. He had a confused glimpse of Milla beating back three or four guardsmen, jumping between pieces of furniture. Then Ranil pushed his head into the floor and Tal couldn't see any more.

Tal heard another exchange of blows, the sharp ring of metal and the strangely mellow note of steel striking the Merwin horn. One guard yelled and another yelped in pain. "Back!" commanded a guard and there was a rush of feet.

Tal made a superhuman effort, every muscle in his back straining, and twisted round. He saw ash swirling in circles, guards leaping back, Milla jumping from the top of a cupboard. Then a great blue electric spark shot from the hand of one of the guards, straight into Milla's chest. There was a crack like thunder, a brilliant flash and the thud of Milla's body hitting the floor.

"That got it, whatever it was," said a guard, relief in his voice. There was a murmur of agreement.

Tal closed his eyes in total shock.

Milla was dead.

They had come so far and survived so much. He couldn't believe that it was all going to end here. Here in Ebbitt's dusty corridor.

Tal saw Milla's face, laughing as she told him they had to jump back across that dreadful chasm. Milla, who should have lived to become a Shield Maiden and have songs sung of her exploits. Now the Far Raiders would never even know what had become of their bravest daughter.

Rough hands rolled Tal over and someone took the chain and his ruined Sunstone out of his hand. Tal opened his eyes as the guard searched him for weapons.

Everything had gone wrong in an instant. It was all over, not just for Milla, but for Tal, his family, everyone.

The guard's Spiritshadow knelt next to Tal's head, ready to grab him if he moved. The other claw held Tal's shadowguard up by the scruff of its neck. Once again it had taken the shape of a Dattu.

"You're Tal Graile-Rerem?" asked a voice, someone

outside Tal's field of vision. He started to turn his head, but stopped when the Spiritshadow's clawed hands closed around his neck.

"Yes," he muttered dully. He could hardly be bothered to hide the Sunstone in his cheek. Nothing mattered anymore. He had failed and Milla was dead.

"It's him," confirmed another voice. "I saw him play Beastmaker. Why does Sushin want him?"

Shadowmaster Sushin remained Tal's enemy, though he didn't know why. Bleakly Tal wondered how Sushin – who was only a Brightstar of the Orange – had the power to send Imperial Guards after Tal. And why would he bother?

"Where did that other one come from, Tal?" asked the guard who'd questioned his identity. "From the Underfolk depths? Who made the sword for her?"

"She was my guest," mumbled Tal mechanically. His voice seemed to come from far away, as if it weren't really him speaking. "Milla. She is... she was an Icecarl. From outside."

Silence greeted this answer, as the guards

stopped what they were doing. Then there was a nervous sort of half laugh and a cough before they all started moving again.

"Outside? What do you mean, *outside*?"

"Outside the Castle," said Tal. "From the Ice."

"You expect us to believe that?" asked the guard. She sounded angry now.

"No," replied Tal bitterly. "But it's true."

"Take them away," ordered the guard. "Tal to the Pit. The girl to the Hall of Nightmares. Let Fashnek get the truth out of her. And no one is to speak of this. Understood?"

There was a chorus of agreement and a sudden bustle of activity.

For a few seconds the full meaning of what the guard had said didn't sink in. The words slowly repeated over and over in his head.

*The girl to the Hall of Nightmares.*

He felt like a four-year-old struggling to read. Then it hit him, all at once.

Milla must be alive! They wouldn't take a corpse to answer questions in the Hall of Nightmares!

Tal found a tiny spark of hope light up the darkness inside him, but it did not lift it completely. Milla might be alive, but both of them were in terrible danger, Milla perhaps most of all.

The Hall of Nightmares was a place where Spiritshadows could enter your dreams and change them into nightmares. It was the place where Chosen who transgressed the Empress's laws were punished. For Milla, who had the Icecarls' loathing of free shadows, it would be absolutely terrifying.

Tal gasped as a Spiritshadow suddenly wound itself round him, securing his arms and legs, then extending a thin tentacle across his eyes. It felt something like his own shadowguard, but not entirely, like putting on a familiar shirt that was unexpectedly damp. It was also strong enough to completely bind him and he could see nothing through its shadow-flesh blindfold.

Only then did he think about what was going to happen to him. Milla was going to the Hall of Nightmares, but he was being taken to the Pit.

Tal had never even heard of the Pit.

# 13

Milla had been blinded and knocked out by the blast from the guard's Sunstone. Only her face mask and armour had saved her from being burned, and they were both charred, the amber lenses of the mask partly melted and the Selski hide black and peeling.

The guards had quickly stripped the armour and mask off and tied her wrists and ankles. Shrouding her in a tablecloth taken from Ebbitt's hoard, they rushed her away, taking the least-travelled corridors to the Hall of Nightmares.

Even so, people saw them, and many Chosen would later remark on the four dishevelled, bruised and bleeding guards, and the body they carried between them. But all thought they were simply disposing of an Underfolk who had run amok, which was unusual, but not unheard of.

They did not see Milla's alien white-blonde hair, or the strange clothing she wore. The Merwin sword was also wrapped and could have been any makeshift weapon. One Chosen amused his friends by describing the stupid Underfolk who had gone mad with a table leg.

The guards were unlucky in one shortcut they chose. The Middle Garden was a large, open chamber of high-vaulted ceilings, restful tree ferns, reflective pools lined with small Sunstones and crystal fountains that grew of their own accord and then collapsed to grow again.

It was unusual for more than four moody Chosen to be there. But that particular day, Brightstar Parl of the Blue was re-creating to forty-seven of his closest friends the Achievement of Poetry that had won him the Violet Ray of Attainment.

Parl was reciting his poem and writing all three hundred and eighty words of it in letters of acrobatic blue light when the guards came running through, completely putting him off. He faltered in mid stanza and the blue-light letters crashed into one another, producing a rather disgusting, lumpy cloud of greenish-brown that hung over the audience.

The onlookers took a moment to realise what had happened. As they did, they turned their Sunstones on the guards, flashing Red Rays of Dissatisfaction to show their displeasure at the insult to Parl's work of genius.

While the Chosen would do no more than this, their Spiritshadows reflected their masters' true feelings, looming up from the floor to make aggressive gestures at the guards.

The guards did not stop to offer Blue Rays of Respectful Apology. The audience was left to mutter and complain, while Parl collapsed sobbing, adding his tears to one of the Sunstone-filled pools.

Once clear of the Middle Garden, there were no more obstacles – only single Chosen who rapidly got out of their way. The Hall of Nightmares was located on the eastern side of the Castle, in an area of many empty rooms and chambers. Chosen did not go there, unless it was against their will. Most would only reluctantly admit that the Hall of Nightmares even existed.

Unlike most doors in the Castle, which were marked with the colour of the Order and a family sign or official notice, the great gate to the Hall of Nightmares was completely white. It was securely shut, with a single Sunstone where the keyhole would normally be.

The guards lowered Milla's unconscious body to the floor, then one touched his Sunstone bracelet to the stone in the door. Violet light flashed and the gate slowly groaned open. There was nothing but darkness beyond.

"One for you, Fashnek!" shouted a guard nervously. They made no attempt to pass through the gate.

Footsteps sounded in the hall beyond and the guards moved back.

Slow footsteps, as if the walker found moving difficult or struggled with a great weight.

The guards shuffled even further back as the

yet-unseen Fashnek emerged into the light – and the reason for their fear became obvious.

Fashnek was a tall, very thin man with long black hair tied back behind his head. His most distinctive feature should have been his broad nose with its widely flared nostrils, as if he smelled his way through life.

But when he stepped out into the light, all eyes were drawn to the left side of his body, because most of it was missing. Something had chewed on him from hip to shoulder and his left arm was not human.

The missing flesh had been replaced by shadow. Night-dark pincers flexed at the end of his new left arm. It too was made of shadow, and jointed in three places.

Even worse than the shadow filling in missing flesh, the rest of the Spiritshadow was joined to Fashnek like a bonded twin. It had filled Fashnek's missing body where it could, but was unable to significantly alter its own shape.

It had an insectoid form, with six multijointed limbs, a bulbous body and a head with a long mouth like the neck of a bottle. The end of this hideous mouth was completely ringed with tiny curved teeth, disturbingly like a grossly enlarged leech. To keep Fashnek's appearance as human as it could, the Spiritshadow clung to his side and back, hiding as much as possible behind him.

Kept alive in such an appalling way, Fashnek was repulsive to other Chosen. He could never be welcomed to any Attainment, entertainment or event. He could never be seen at the Empress's court or in the Assembly.

But he had found his place in the Hall of Nightmares.

And now the others feared him. Reaching down with human hand and shadow-flesh pincer, he gripped the tablecloth and slowly pulled Milla's unconscious body into the Hall.

As Milla's heels passed the gate, it slowly ground shut. The guards, who had watched in silence, didn't move until a loud click pronounced the doors locked once more.

# 14

Milla regained consciousness, instantly appraising her situation as she had been trained to do. This was not easy, since she was in total darkness. But she could still hear and smell. So she lay where she was, reaching out with senses made sharper without sight, while she went over what had happened.

She remembered Tal shouting at her to run. Then she had wounded one of the enemy in the arm. She wasn't sure what happened after that.

Clearly she had been captured. But she was not tied up, as she would have been by an enemy Icecarl clan. The Chosen might have other ways to restrain her.

Moving slowly and surreptitiously, Milla touched the floor. It was some sort of smooth, cool material, not stone or bone. The only things she could compare it to were the crystal ladder in the heating tunnels or the pyramid of Imrir.

Milla extended her arms, feeling with her fingertips. The floor started to curve up not very far out. It took Milla only a few seconds to work out that she was contained inside a globe. A crystal globe.

It was large enough for her to sit up, but she couldn't stand. And despite the absence of holes, fresh air somehow got in.

The situation appeared even worse than the plight of the legendary Ulla Strong-Arm, who had been swallowed by an ancient, broken-jawed Selski and had to cut her way free from its stomach. She had supposedly never eaten Selski meat again after that.

Crouching, Milla sniffed the air once more. As she thought, there was the hint of fresh air and the faintest draft. The globe must have tiny holes. She could smell dust too, and at least one person. Sweat hung rank in the air. "So you have woken, Underfolk," said a voice in the darkness.

Milla moved to face the voice, calmly and slowly, as befitted a Shield Maiden. She had already begun the Rovkir-breathing, the steady intake and exhalation of breath that helped keep her fear under control.

*A Shield Maiden should fear, for fear is human*, she recited mentally. *But a Shield Maiden must not show fear, nor let it rule her.*

"I am not an Underfolk," she said aloud. "I am an Icecarl. Free me from this cage and I will fight you."

"An Icecarl?" asked the voice. "You have an imagination. That is rare in Underfolk."

Milla did not answer. She closed her fists instead and pushed them together. Breath came and went, and she slowly tensed and relaxed every muscle in her body, starting from her toes. Breathing caused a surprising amount of pain due to the bruises, burns and dull ache in her side where the Merwin had struck her.

"Is that what you dream of?" asked the voice. "You invent yourself another life where you are not just an Underfolk of the Castle. Well, let us see."

A faint hissing sound came from near Milla's

feet. Instantly she jumped up, pressing her hands and feet against the globe to lift herself off the floor. It was not some sort of shadow coming in, as she'd feared. A sickly sweet smell attacked her nostrils.

Bad air, thought Milla, and she held her breath. But not bad air like in the heating tunnels. This smelled of cooking and metal. Instinctively she knew people had made it.

Light was beginning to blossom around the globe. Sunstones were sparking into life. Different-coloured stones shone focused rays into the globe rather than diffusing light all around.

In the light of seven different colours, Milla could see that the crystal of the globe contained thousands of thin silver wires. The rays from the Sunstones hit these wires and sent light shooting through them, making a complex pattern whirl round and round the globe.

She also saw a coloured mist slowly rising from the base of the globe, so she kept holding her breath. The coloured lights were doing something to her though. She could feel them as well as see them, even with her eyes closed. It felt as if they touched nerves under her skin. Her teeth ached and it felt as if thousands of sharp needles were pricking all over her legs and arms.

She saw the Spiritshadow and the man it was connected to. They were approaching the globe, hobbling together. It was as if the worst of the Mother Crones' cautionary tales had come alive in front of her. A shadow had overcome a man and absorbed him.

Shocked, she took a sudden, short breath. Even as she realised her mistake, the sweet smoke was entering her lungs. Milla felt dizzy and very, very tired. She slid slowly down the globe until she was once more resting on the bottom.

Her eyes closed and she drifted into sleep.

Fashnek touched the globe. His Spiritshadow arm slowly pushed through the crystal. The pincer opened and extended itself around Milla's head. But the pincer did not close.

Fashnek smiled. Using his human hand, he raised a Sunstone. He concentrated on it and it flashed with light. The other Sunstones all around flashed too, filling the globe with swirling colours.

Fashnek shut his eyes and entered Milla's dreams.

# 15

Tal's first reaction to the Pit was relief that it wasn't the Hall of Nightmares. As he'd been carried through the back corridors of the Castle, he'd had plenty of time to imagine what the Pit might be like. His mind had flooded with possibilities, like a pit filled with water, where he'd have to swim constantly to avoid drowning.

But that would probably have been called the Pool. So he started to think of things that might be kept in pits. A rogue Spiritshadow perhaps? The Pit would have to be kept in total darkness or lined with mirrors to hold the Spiritshadow in there, but it was certainly possible.

It was only since he had met the Icecarls that Tal had even considered the concept of a rogue Spiritshadow. The idea had lingered like a dark seed in his brain and it was now in full flower. He could imagine something uncurling in a dark corner, slowly reaching out to grab him while he lay tied up and unable to move. It would speak to him constantly, in a voice that would be the voice of the Keeper from the Red Tower, high and horrible...

By the time they actually got to the Pit, Tal was sick with fear. He could barely breathe and he had cramps in his stomach. His hands were twitching uncontrollably, like a light-puppet performance gone wrong.

When the Spiritshadow unpeeled itself from his eyes, Tal had to call on all his courage to look at what was awaiting him. But the Pit was just a pit. A circular shaft about fifteen stretches in diameter and maybe thirty stretches deep. There was no sign of anything waiting in it.

But as the Spiritshadow stepped back from him, Tal had another awful second in which he imagined a previously unconsidered possibility:

they were going to push him in, and he would break his legs and lie there in agony until he died. Instinctively he looked for his shadowguard. It was still in the grip of the Spiritshadow.

The guards took a step forward. Tal gulped out of nervousness, stopping himself just in time to avoid swallowing the Sunstone.

But they didn't push him in. They stopped a few paces from him, with their Spiritshadows between them, and raised their Sunstones. Violet rays rushed out, forming one broad beam that wrapped itself round Tal. His own Sunstone answered, so he had to quickly turn his head away from the guards to hide the light shining through his cheek and leaking through his tightly closed lips.

The Violet beam slowly took on a shape, turning into an enormous hand of light. It closed its fingers around Tal and suddenly he was lifted into the air, his head almost smacking into the ceiling.

The guards had created a Hand of Light. Tal knew it was possible, but he had never seen it in practice. It took several Chosen of great skill and powerful Sunstones acting together. Of course, the guards were all members of the Violet Order, and were therefore among the most proficient users of Light magic in the Castle.

"Time for a little dance?" asked one guard, and the others laughed. The Hand immediately shook Tal from side to side and then up and down, until he felt sick.

Because he had the Sunstone in his mouth, Tal couldn't scream or beg for mercy. This made the game boring for the guards, who soon lost interest. The Hand stopped its wild movements and quickly lowered Tal down to the bottom of the Pit.

It let him go there, hovered just above his headand waved its luminous fingers in farewell, accompanied by more laughter from the guards. Then it shrank away into nothing as the four Chosen ceased concentrating on their Sunstones.

As the Hand disappeared, so did the light. Tal was left in semidarkness. The room above the Pit was lit by Sunstones, but very little of their light came down the deep hole to Tal. He was tempted to use his own stone, but there was a chance the guards hadn't gone very far. They would take it from him if it was discovered.

He could still see enough to explore what little there was at the bottom of the Pit. He was glad to see a mouldy but serviceable mattress against one wall, and even more pleased to find that there was a small pool of water, fed by a pipe. On the other side of the Pit, there was a primitive toilet, just a narrow sewer that went straight down. It was too narrow to escape through, even if he could stand it.

There was also a basket in the corner, with half of a very stale loaf of bread in it. Tal took this as sign that food would probably be provided.

He sat down on the mattress and spat the Sunstone into his hand. Then he slipped it into his sleeve pocket. He was still wearing his Icecarl furs, though his big outer coat had been left at the entrance to the heatway tunnels. Even the inner furs were too warm, quite smelly and uncomfortable.

As his eyes adjusted to the dim light, Tal sat and thought about his situation. He was well aware that he had done things that were not the actions of a proper Chosen. But even though he had probably broken a dozen laws, he wasn't supposed to be punished like this.

According to what he'd learned in the Lectorium, a Chosen couldn't be taken to a place like the Hall of Nightmares until they'd had a trial, and even after that they could appeal to the Assembly of the Chosen, or to the Empress.

He should have been brought before the Lumenor of the Orange Order first and then been tried in the Old Court. He should have a Speaker for the Accused, an older Chosen with an interest in law, to represent him.

*What was going on?*

Tal sighed and bent his head. There were too many problems confronting him. He still hadn't seen his mother, let alone helped her. Gref was lost. Kusi was in the clutches of the ghastly cousins.

And Milla was in the Hall of Nightmares. She wouldn't even know what was going to happen to her there. Unlike Tal, who had heard awful stories about the Hall of Nightmares all his life. It was the worst punishment he could imagine.

Spiritshadows would enter Milla's dreams.

They would change them into nightmares, nightmares that she would be unable to escape. She wouldn't be able to wake up until they let her.

Tal had seen what the Hall of Nightmares did to rebellious Underfolk. For years the same man had worked in the main passage outside Tal's family chambers. He was a sweeper and cleaner. One day he started throwing soapy water at passing Chosen, then the actual buckets, and a Half-Bright was knocked unconscious. The Underfolk was taken away to the Hall of Nightmares. When he came back, he shook and shivered for weeks and no longer smiled as the Chosen children played their games with light and shadow in the hallways.

He was one of the lucky ones.

Some never came back at all.

Tal didn't want to see Milla like that. Which meant that he had to rescue her. Then find the Codex, so he could find Gref. Then get his mother to Aenir, so she could be cured. *Then* clear his name, so he could become a proper Chosen. And *then* find a Sunstone for the Far Raiders as he'd promised.

"One step at a time," Tal whispered. His father

had always said that, when Tal complained about everything he had to do.

He suddenly remembered his father and mother helping Kusi to walk for the first time. They had stood on either side of the smiling baby, holding her hands, with Gref and Tal walking backwards in front of her. "One step at a time," they'd all chanted, and Kusi had taken her first step, and then another and another...

Tal's first step had to be to get out of the Pit. He couldn't do anything from a hole in the ground. He looked at the triple scar on his wrist, where he had been marked by the Crone. Something of the Icecarls must have got into him. Like the Icecarls, and the Selski they followed, Tal knew that if he stopped, he would die.

Having made the decision to escape, Tal put on the Sunstone ring, turning the stone inwards so he could shield it with his hand. Then he called forth a very faint light and used it to search around the sides of the Pit. He had learned to climb well on the Mountain of Light. If there were any cracks in the wall he might be able to climb up, using them as toe- and fingerholds.

But the walls were smooth and seamless. By the time Tal had been halfway around he knew it was useless. The Pit hadn't been dug with normal tools, but cut through solid rock with Light, probably by Chosen using Sunstones. The walls were as smooth as glass, the rock actually fused.

He was about to give up when he noticed a small rough patch, right at eye level. Nothing that would help him climb, but Tal rushed over for a closer look anyway.

The roughness was not an accident. Someone had scratched letters and numbers into the rock. Several different people, Tal thought, from the variations in handwriting. Some scratches were faded and clearly very old. Some were obviously fresher. There were fragments of names, and tally-marks that probably counted meals, for there would be no other way of keeping time. Unlike the Icecarls, Chosen did not care to count every breath, unconsciously or otherwise.

There had been prisoners who'd spent months here, or even years.

Was there *any* way to escape?

# 16

There were at least twenty names scratched into the stone. Tal held his Sunstone close, puzzling them out. None of the names were familiar to him, until he came to one of the most recent, down at the bottom.

When he saw it, he felt his skin go cold and his breath stop. He bent even closer, unable to believe it. Then he touched the stone, hoping the scratched letters might disappear under his fingertips.

But they didn't and no matter how Tal looked they still spelled out the same name. And he recognised the distinctive curve of the letters.

*Rerem.*

Tal's father. He had been here. In the Pit. That

meant that he *hadn't* disappeared on a secret mission for the Empress as Sushin had said. He had been kept here, until he had escaped... or something else had happened to him.

Tal shivered. He didn't want to think about anything but escape. His father was smarter and stronger than he was. He would have escaped. That was why he hadn't been able to come home. The enemies who had imprisoned him here would have been looking for him. He must be hiding somewhere, waiting for an opportunity to get word to the Empress or his friends.

That would be difficult, since some of the Imperial Guard were clearly involved with Rerem's enemies. A terrible plot was under way, though Tal couldn't imagine what that plot involved. Rerem must have discovered something and that was why they wanted Tal imprisoned too.

Tal felt certain that Shadowmaster Sushin was behind it all. Tal remembered how he'd enjoyed telling Tal that his father was dead and then giving him the deluminents. Tal looked at his wrist and laughed. The crystal bracelets marking him for demotion were long gone, lost in the fall from the Red Tower. He'd probably be given even more for losing the first lot. Perhaps even a full seven and an instant demotion to the Red Order. Or even fourteen and a welcome to the ranks of the Underfolk.

Tal didn't care about deluminents any more. Whoever his enemy was, Sushin or someone else, they didn't care about following the rules and laws of the Chosen. So Tal wouldn't either.

Defiantly, he scratched his own name under his father's, using the same worn metal spoon that the others must have used. There was hardly any of it left; certainly it was of no use as a weapon.

Tal had just finished when he heard movement up above. Not the solid crash of the guards' boots, but a more slithery sound. Hastily, Tal dimmed his Sunstone and put it back in his pocket. Then he lay down on the mouldy mattress and pretended to be asleep.

Looking up at the pale opening of the Pit, Tal saw a Spiritshadow peering over the edge – a tall, horned creature that rested its clawed forelegs on the lip of the Pit as if it might jump down. Tal kept his eyes on it and very slowly reached into his pocket for the Sunstone, his heart racing. If it did jump, he would blast it. Or try to.

But the Spiritshadow turned away. It was replaced by a Chosen, a glittering figure wreathed in light by the many Sunstones on his rings, chain and staff. The staff was one that belonged to a Deputy Lumenor, with the orange glow that marked him as of the Orange Order – Tal's own Order.

For a moment, Tal thought that everything was going to be set right. The Deputy Lumenor had come to release him. The guards and the other plotters would already be in the Old Court, facing up to their crimes.

Tal then realised that the Chosen above was not Neril, the Deputy Lumenor he knew, who had held the post for many, many years. It was someone else, someone taller and broader, lit so brightly that Tal couldn't see his or her face.

Then the Deputy Lumenor spoke and Tal's hopes were destroyed. He knew that voice.

It was Shadowmaster Sushin. Somehow he had been promoted to Deputy Lumenor of the Orange Order. And to Brightblinder, judging from the new, larger chain of Sunstones he wore round his neck.

But that wasn't possible, or at least it wasn't according to what Tal had been taught. Brightstar was the highest rank in the Orange Order. To go higher you had to be in the Green Order at least. However he did it, Sushin seemed expert at getting promotions and titles, since he was a Shadowmaster too, which was a title given directly by the Empress and usually went with a particular office or job. Sushin had never mentioned what that was.

"Young Tal," said Sushin, in the tone of voice a lector might use if he found his students somewhere they weren't supposed to be.

"What happened to Neril?" asked Tal, unable to keep the anger from his voice. "The proper Deputy Lumenor?"

"No, no," said Sushin. "That is no way to begin. Surely you have not forgotten all your manners, wherever you might have been."

"I haven't forgotten," replied Tal, but he made no move to get up and bow. "And even if I had a Sunstone I wouldn't offer light to you."

"Really?" asked Sushin dryly. "You are a rude boy."

He held up a chain and the light from his

Sunstones dimmed. Even so, it took Tal's eyes a moment to adjust and see what it was. His own chain and the blackened remnant of his old Sunstone.

"What happened to your Sunstone?" asked Sushin.

"None of your business," said Tal.

"But it *is* my business," Sushin explained. "You see, without a Sunstone, you are not a Chosen, Tal."

*Not a Chosen*. The words went through Tal like a Merwin horn. He was caught now. If he admitted he had a new Sunstone, it would probably be taken away. If he didn't, Sushin could treat him like an Underfolk.

"As Deputy Lumenor of the Orange Order," the Shadowmaster continued, "I have to discover whether your loss was an accident, in which case the stone should be replaced, or whether it was deliberate destruction. In the latter case, your demotion to Underfolk would be immediate, as would other... punishments."

Tal didn't reply. He knew Sushin was just playing with him. The Shadowmaster was his enemy.

"I can replace your Sunstone," said Sushin. He reached into his pocket and pulled out a bright new chain of gold, with a large Sunstone set as the pendant. "A Primary Sunstone, Tal. Strong enough to take you and your family into Aenir on the Day of Ascension. The day when you become a full Chosen... or not. I understand that getting to Aenir is particularly important for your mother at the moment. Or so my dear friends Lallek and Korrek tell me. They are so concerned about your family."

Tal looked at the Sunstone. It dangled loosely in Sushin's puffy fingers, as if he might drop it down at any moment.

"What about Gref?" asked Tal. "What have you done to him?"

"He could be found," Sushin replied, not really answering the question.

"What... what would I have to do?" Tal asked, his voice cracking. If he got the Sunstone and was reinstated in the Orange Order, Gref would be brought home and together they could take care of their mother. Later he could try to help Milla, find out what was going on and discover what had happened to his father.

But could he trust Sushin?

# 17

"You must answer my questions, to begin with," Sushin said. "You were climbing the outside of the Red Tower and you fell. Yet here you are. How? Who helped you?"

"The Icecarls," Tal told him.

Sushin sighed, and his Spiritshadow loomed threateningly over the edge.

"I want the names of the Chosen," said the Shadowmaster. "Not stories, and not your senile great-uncle Ebbitt. Someone helped you escape the Red Tower, someone with real power. Someone hid you these last few weeks. Tell me their names."

"No one," replied Tal. "I was taken by the

wind, far from the Castle. The Icecarls found—"

"I said *I do not want stories*!" shouted Sushin. He raised his hand and a bolt of concentrated light shot out, striking the corner of the mattress, setting it alight. Tal rolled away, covering his eyes with his forearm. His shadowguard scuttled after him, spreading itself wide to shield him from the attack.

As Tal rolled, he saw Sushin throw another bolt. His Spiritshadow was behind him, its claws striking at the air, its huge fanged mouth snapping as if it might already have Tal in its jaws.

Tal suddenly realised that Sushin's Spiritshadow shouldn't be a fanged claw-beast. Last time he'd seen Sushin, his Spiritshadow had a domed shell and a long flat head. Spiritshadows could stretch and spread, but they couldn't completely change shape!

So Sushin must have got a completely new Spiritshadow. He must have gone into Aenir before the Day of Ascension. That was totally forbidden.

For a very long minute, Sushin threw bolts of white-hot light down at Tal. The boy ducked and weaved, but in the narrow confines of the Pit he knew he would be hit soon. His shadowguard had already deflected one bolt and now had a rip through its shadowflesh that would take days to heal. Finally Sushin calmed down and the bolts stopped. Tal stopped running, though his body was still tensed to jump aside.

"Who is the girl who was captured with you?" Sushin demanded. "Where did she steal her weapon? Are there other Underfolk who helped you?"

"Her name is Milla," said Tal. He didn't know how to answer the other questions. Clearly Sushin thought that Tal had used Light magic to fly down the Red Tower and then had hidden with renegade Underfolk in the lower levels.

"She's an Icecarl!" he shouted, jumping away from the expected bolt of light.

But Sushin didn't raise his hand. He said, "The Pit is a good place to think, Tal. You should remember that the only way out is to give the right answers. To me."

He turned to leave. Tal sighed with relief and looked down. In that instant, Sushin turned back and fired a final bolt. It struck the ground at Tal's feet, sparks flying up to strafe his legs. He was knocked down, his shadowguard cushioning his fall.

On his back, with his shadowguard under him, Tal could only look up as Sushin pointed his Sunstone-ring hand at him. He lay there, waiting for the killing bolt, but Sushin only laughed and turned away. This time he did not come back.

Tal lay there for a long time, until his shadowguard crept out from under him and started tugging at his foot. Wearily, the boy sat up and looked at his legs. The bolt had burned all the fur off his leggings, revealing the hide underneath. Sparks had burned through to scorch his skin in a few spots. But it wasn't serious.

Tal laughed. A month ago he would have gone straight to bed for a week with these tiny burns. Now he had grown closer to Icecarl standards. The burns were annoying, nothing more.

Getting to his feet, he went over to the water basin, stripped off his furs and washed himself as best he could. He kept the clothes close, in case he heard Sushin returning.

Tal was just slipping his leggings back on when

he heard footsteps again. Quickly he threw on his coat and retreated to the far side.

But it wasn't Sushin. Or at least it didn't sound like him. Whoever it was didn't slide his or her feet. Again it didn't sound like a guard's heavy boots.

Tal tensed as a shadow slid over the rim of the Pit. Then he relaxed. It was a natural shadow and the person who cast it was close behind, in the white robe of an Underfolk.

An old woman, Tal saw, though she didn't meet his eyes. She knelt at the edge of the Pit and carefully lowered a basket down on a very thin rope, sufficient to support the basket, but not Tal if he tried to grab it. When the basket hit the bottom, she kept lowering, till the hook on the rope swung clear and she hauled it back up again very quickly.

Stale bread, Tal thought gloomily. The Underfolk woman pointed at it and said something very quietly, then she quickly walked away.

It wasn't until she'd gone that Tal managed to work out that she'd said, "Compliments of your great-uncle."

Even with those words, Tal waited until he could no longer hear footsteps. Then he went over to the basket and lifted its lid.

Delightful aromas escaped and Tal's mouth was suddenly no longer dry. There was half a fresh-baked pie, spiced with menahas sprigs, and two seed cakes. A stone bottle contained cold sweetwater.

Even though he was suddenly hungry, it was not the food and drink that most attracted Tal's attention. In one corner of the basket, there was a clump of pages. Judging from the torn stitching and absence of binding, it had been ripped from the middle of a book. Tal picked it up and saw that he only held a few chapters. It started at page 173 and ended in midsentence on page 215.

The first line was, "On Making a Stairway of Light."

# 18

Milla woke on the deck of an iceship. For a moment she was disoriented, then she felt the familiar bone under her feet and the wind in her hair. She heard the screech of the ship's runners on the ice.

But something was not quite right. She looked down at herself and saw that she was not dressed in the full furs she should be wearing on deck. And her Merwin-horn sword was gone, as was her knife and throwing crescent. How could she have been so careless as to come on deck unclothed and unarmed?

The colour of the Sunstone on the mast was wrong. It had an unpleasant greenish tint that made the Ice look sickly. And there was no one else on deck. Which was impossible. There was always a watch on deck...

Milla looked around. There was no obvious sign of an enemy, but she felt an unwelcome presence. She slowly went to lower her mask. But it wasn't there either. Puzzled, Milla ran her hands over her hair, which was strangely long. No mask, no weapons, no outer furs, long hair.

The wind was howling through the rigging. The sails were full, the ship speeding across the ice. But Milla did not feel cold.

Milla knew there could only be one explanation for this. She must be dreaming.

There was no point trying to wake up from inside a dream. When her time came she would wake. She took a deep, slow breath and sat down, drawing her legs up underneath her. Then she bent forward and laid her forehead on the deck, between her spread palms. She began to breathe in the Fourth Rovkir Pattern, which would send her into an even deeper level of consciousness, deeper and further down than dreams.

She didn't hear the creatures that came swarming over the sides of the ship, or feel their jaws and claws upon her. She didn't notice them disappear, or see the ship hit a huge rock and go into a cartwheeling explosion. She didn't see the Spiritshadows that rushed at her, intent on ripping her dream-self apart.

Milla had already left that dream-body. She had gone further, so far that she had lost her identity. She was a tiny glowing spark in a great void of nothingness that would hide until she was found by someone with the power to return her to her dream-body and then to her physical form.

Two different people were alerted by what Milla had done. One was close to her physically and was puzzled – perhaps a little afraid. The other one was physically far away and merely curious.

The first was Fashnek, master of the Hall of Nightmares. He had gone into Milla's dream and seen the iceship. That had been Milla's dreaming. But when Fashnek began to change it, sending monsters to attack, Milla's dream-shape had not responded as an Underfolk or a Chosen would. She should have run screaming and crying, trying to wake up. But she had stayed completely still and uncaring, and the monsters could not touch her.

Fashnek had put a great rock in the ship's path and destroyed the vessel in the crash. But still Milla's dream-shape had not been touched. The piece of deck she lay on had simply sailed through the air and landed perfectly on the Ice.

Fashnek had called on his own and other Spiritshadows then, bringing them directly into her dream. Even they could not touch her. Their shadow-claws and teeth simply passed through the dream girl. She did not respond in any way.

Fashnek became angry. He retreated back into his damaged flesh, to change the settings of the Sunstones, to focus more power on the prisoner in the crystal globe. He sent a message too, advising his own master that he had found someone whose dreams resisted his power.

While he was out of Milla's dream, another person entered it. She came skating across the ice, though her boots had no skates, and with each sliding footstep she moved further than any real skater could. She wore no furs, just a plain black robe. Her eyes shone like stars and her long hair was as white as the ice. Tal would have recognised her as the Crone of the Far Raiders. Here in Milla's dream she was younger and taller by half a stretch.

She looked at the wreckage and sniffed at the ice around Milla's bent-over dream body. Whatever she smelled made her nose wrinkle. She did not touch Milla, but turned away and shouted out into the darkness. The shout shattered the ice in front of her and sent pieces of bone debris flying into the air.

The shout was answered almost immediately. More black-robed figures came skating in over the Ice. More star-eyed Crones, arriving in twos and threes until forty of them clustered close. They did not speak, but gathered round Milla's dream body, waiting for someone.

Eventually that someone came. A Crone Mother, milky-eyed, seated in a high-backed chair of palest bone. The chair moved across the Ice of its own accord. It stopped next to Milla and the Crone Mother bent down and touched the girl's head.

Milla came back from wherever she had been to

find herself still in a dream. She knew it was a dream because of all the Crones around her and the Crone Mother in her chair of bone. They were the familiar figures of her childhood, the Crones who came to send the nightmares away. All Icecarl children learned how to cope with nightmares, how to move within their dreams and when to call the Crones.

As always, the Crones did not speak. But they didn't throw Milla up into the air either, which was how they normally woke her up. The Crone Mother smiled at her and did not remove her hand. All the other Crones stood in a circle round her, looking out, still waiting.

They did not have to wait long.

Fashnek re-entered Milla's dream. As he usually did in his prisoners' dreams, he made himself look like he had once been, before the accident that left him only half-alive. It was only in others' dreams that Fashnek could bear to look at himself.

The Chosen was surprised to see all the weird women in black circled round Milla. The ancient globe and its associated devices – which he fondly called his Nightmare machines – were set to prevent the dreamer from changing the dream. Fashnek was the only one who could do that. But the machines were as old as the Castle and soaked up Light magic like a sponge drank water.

Sometimes a Sunstone would fail during an interrogation and the dreamer would have a little bit of freedom to invent things.

Not that it mattered. Fashnek was sure that he could make this one respond now. He had replaced all the Sunstones. The crystal globe and the mind boosters were all functioning at full power.

First, he would change the place back to something she hadn't dreamed herself. A place where he had more control. Like the Hunting Arena, where Chosen chased and killed rock lizards. He would change this girl into a lizard as well.

Fashnek thought of the changes he wanted. Transmitted by his Spiritshadow to the Nightmare machines, the changes should have been immediate. But they weren't. The Ice flickered for a moment and Fashnek briefly saw the bright green of the ferns and the red flash of a lizard's back. Then it was gone and the Ice returned.

Fashnek frowned. A whole lot of Sunstones must have failed. He concentrated on the change again, but nothing happened.

Then he noticed that the creepy old women

were sliding towards him, sliding across the ice in a way that was not possible. They were dream elements. They shouldn't be able to do anything without his permission.

They were all staring at him too. Staring with luminous eyes, eyes that were not merely reflecting the light from Fashnek's Sunstones, or the one in the wreckage of the ship.

"Back!" Fashnek ordered, speaking aloud to reinforce his mental command. But they still came on, closer and closer.

Fashnek started to retreat, fear building inside him. This was all wrong. Prisoners came to the Hall of Nightmares to be made afraid by Fashnek. He controlled their dreams, not the other way around.

The gliding women drew knives of bone. Fashnek shivered when he saw them. He tried desperately to order Spiritshadows to come to his aid. None came. He conjured up monsters he had used before, things from Beastmaker games. None came.

Soon he was surrounded. There was only one thing left to do. Fashnek ordered the Nightmare machine to switch off and made himself wake up.

He disappeared. The Crones tucked their knives away and skated back to Milla. She had watched them chase the Chosen away. She knew who he was, even though he appeared whole, here in her dream. He was her jailer. In the waking world, she was trapped inside a crystal globe. But at least he could not interfere with her dreams.

The Crone Mother took her hand off Milla's head as the others returned. They circled round Milla, towering over her. She was puzzled for a moment, until she realised that their size had been set when she first learned to call them to her nightmares. She had seen only five circlings then, and stood only waist-high. The Crones had always been double her size. Now that she was grown, in her dream they had grown too.

The Crones picked her up. They held her over their heads, supported on a forest of old arms. Then they bounced her up and down a few times, making her laugh.

On the third bounce, they threw her up into the dark sky with all the strength they could muster. Milla flew, tumbling over and over, laughing at the rush and giddiness. It was like falling up forever.

Then there was a flash of light.

Milla woke up. She was still trapped in the crystal globe. Multicoloured beams of light were still focused on her, but now they were just light. They had lost their effect upon her. Fresh air breezed through the globe, unaccompanied by the sickly sweet scent.

There was no sign of Fashnek. He had hurried off to report in person. He had to report that the boy Tal had not been lying. This girl truly was from outside the Castle, and she had powers and allies that made Fashnek sweat and tremble as he lay at the feet of his master.

It took Tal four hours to read the section of the book he had been given, and then another few hours to read parts of it with greater attention, as he tried to figure out exactly what the author meant. To make it harder, there were pages missing and the section ended with a sentence that began, "The final act to complete the stairway is—"

Tal flipped that final page at least twenty times before he accepted that there were no more. He would have to work out how to finish the stairway on his own.

If he got that far. The stairway used all seven colours of the Spectrum and Tal had only been taught Red, Orange, Yellow and Green. But he had always had a natural flair for Light magic, and both his father and Ebbitt had taught him things he'd never have learned in the Lectorium.

His first small attempts were total failures. The Sunstone was much more powerful than his old one had been and he kept losing control of it. Colours blurred and intensity wavered all over the place. The three stairways he managed to produce all fell over when they were only three or four steps high.

"I can't do it," Tal muttered finally, throwing down the pages. His eyes hurt and he had a headache. He lay down on the mattress and closed his eyes. Just for a few minutes he told himself. Then he would try again.

Before he knew it, Tal was asleep and dreaming. He was out on the Ice again, this time without Milla. But he had a Sunstone, a very bright Sunstone that lit up everything. His shadowguard was there too, but for some reason in the dream he didn't want it. It kept following at his heels and he kept running away from it, slipping and sliding on the Ice. The shadowguard grew bigger and then became Sushin's Spiritshadow. It got larger still, until it filled all the sky behind him, its mouth yawning to swallow him up in a single gulp—

Tal woke with a start, sweating. His shadowguard sat up too, in the shape of a comforting, inoffensive Dattu. Tal looked at his Sunstone. Only twenty minutes had passed.

He splashed his face with water and started working on the Stairway of Light again. This time his focus was more intense.

At first he made a very small stair, just a few steps, carefully weaving different-coloured strands of light together into two short rainbows which he then joined end to end to make three distinct steps.

Even when they hung there in the air, opaque and solid, Tal didn't really believe it would work until he put his foot on the first rainbow step and it supported him.

Elated, he ran up and down the three steps over and over, forgetting that the stairs would only last a few minutes after he stopped concentrating on his Sunstone. They failed just as his right foot came down on the highest step, sending him sprawling. His shadowguard, still repairing itself after Sushin's attack, was too slow to catch him. It hissed in warning – or exasperation – as he picked himself up and limped to the mattress.

A Stairway of Light big enough to get him out of the Pit would take between two and three hours to build, Tal estimated. If he could manage it.

He consulted his Sunstone. It probably hadn't been calibrated by the Timestone in the Assembly for years, but might still be accurate. According to the colour band in its depths, it was close to two o'clock in the morning. It was unlikely that Sushin or anyone else would visit him before the Waking Hour, at seven.

So he had time to escape. But he still hadn't decided if Sushin was being sincere when he offered him a new Sunstone and a safe return to his normal life as a Chosen.

Rubbing his forehead, Tal thought about all this. Eventually he decided that he had to build the stair now and take his chances on escaping. Sushin might be his superior in the Orange Order, but Tal didn't trust him. He'd put Tal in this Pit, after all, so he didn't care about doing things the right way. He might have put Tal's father in this Pit too.

No, Sushin's offer was almost certainly false. He would just get rid of Tal once he found out that he had no allies.

Having made his decision, Tal ignored his headache and started to build the Stairway of Light. There were two methods explained in the book. One was quick and a bit easier, but would use up most of the Sunstone's energy. The other was slower and more difficult, but would not drain the stone too much.

Tal had learned the value of a Sunstone. He chose the slower method, though he got an empty feeling in his stomach as he raised his Sunstone. He would only have one real chance at this. It was a feat of magic that would not usually be attempted by anyone less than a Brightstar of the Blue, and a confident Light Mage at that. Yet here he was, a boy, not even a full Chosen, trying to build a Stairway of Light thirty stretches high!

Step by rainbow step, the stairway started to spiral up and round the Pit. Tal stood in the centre; his Sunstone raised high, sweat beading on his forehead. All his attention was on the stone and the light that poured from it. He had to mentally take each strand and weave it into six others, then when he had the short arc of a rainbow, float it up and attach it to the top of the last one.

When the stairs were only a few stretches short of the top, Tal took a few steps. He had to concentrate so hard on keeping the whole stairway together and on making the last few stairs, that he almost fell off a couple of times.

Finally, the stair was complete. A multicoloured, shimmering spiral of many small rainbows, each one a rounded step of solid light. Tal sighed with relief and climbed up more quickly.

He was three quarters of the way up when he heard the clatter of metal on stone and a voice raised in anger or pain.

Tal was momentarily distracted by the sound and he lost control of his Sunstone. It flared in his hand and a wild beam of multicoloured light shot out.

The beam whipped around and under him, cutting the stairs in half. All the steps below Tal fell apart in a sudden snowstorm of brilliant light. The ones above him changed colour and he felt the step he was on get soft, like melting wax.

Tal threw himself forwards and up, jumping three steps at a time. He didn't even try to fix the stairs. He instinctively knew that whatever had gone wrong was beyond his power to fix. He was also ready for whoever or whatever was waiting for him at the top.

This time he had a Sunstone in his hand and he would fight!

The last step felt like a sponge, but it held long enough for Tal to spring up and out of the Pit. He landed on the edge in a crouch, Sunstone ring held ready, his eyes looking wildly from side to side.

But there was nothing to see. The Pit lay at the end of an otherwise normal Castle corridor. A colourless corridor, whitewashed and lit by regularly spaced Sunstones. There was a door about thirty stretches down the corridor, but that was all.

Except, Tal suddenly noticed, there was a small,

square, dark hole in the ceiling and a metal hatch cover lying on the ground. That was what had made the noise.

Cautiously, Tal crept down the corridor. His every sense was alert for the sudden opening of the door and the rush of guards, or for someone – or something – to drop out of the odd hatch in the ceiling.

As he got closer, Tal heard a weird scuffling sound – whatever was up there was moving around. Then he heard a muffled voice cursing.

It sounded a bit familiar.

"Ebbitt?" asked Tal warily. "Is that you?"

# 21

Tal was answered by a sudden explosion of foul-smelling green water, liberally mixed with what looked and smelled like clumps of rotten spearleaf. This was followed by Ebbitt's head, though it took Tal a moment to recognise him, since his hair was totally sodden and his face was bright green.

"Hurry up!" he said. "I can only hold the water back for a few—"

Whatever he was going to say disappeared into a gurgle as more water suddenly cascaded through the hole. At the same time Tal heard the door at the end of the corridor being unlocked and someone shouting on the other side.

Despite the smell, he jumped up and got a grip on the edge of the hole. Ebbitt helped him get up on to his elbows and then he was able to squirm up the rest of the way.

To Tal's surprise they were in another corridor, rather than some small tunnel. He was even more surprised to see that apart from where they were standing, it was full of water with lots of green floaty things in it. Two walls of light, obviously made by Ebbitt, were keeping the water at bay.

Or most of it. Ebbitt was constantly using his Sunstone to seal off sudden leaks.

"Pow! Kapang! Take that!" he yelled, suppressing three different outbreaks. Then, while the water was momentarily under control, he made a lasso of Indigo light and used it to pull up the metal hatch from the floor. A few seconds later, it was firmly back in place, welded in a sudden flurry of sparks from Ebbitt's Sunstone.

Those few seconds were long enough for Ebbitt's walls to break down. The water came in with a rush, picking up both of them and dumping them down. Filled with sudden panic, Tal struggled to right himself. What if the corridor was entirely full of water and there was nowhere to breathe?

He bobbed to the surface, gasping. Ebbitt was treading water next to him and plucking the rotten plant material off his face. Without a word, he pointed a bony finger past Tal and started to swim in that direction.

Tal followed him with difficulty. He wasn't a great swimmer. Unlike some Chosen of his age, he didn't spend his free time in the Cavern Lakes or the Underfolks' fish pools.

"Thanks, Uncle," he gasped as they swam to wherever it was they were going. Tal couldn't see an end to the corridor. "By the way, where are we?"

"Surge tank, splurge tank, roly-poly nurge tank," said Ebbitt. He stopped swimming to tread water again and said, "When the superheated steam has passed through the heating system it reaches the condenser-menser-spencer, where it's turned back into water-aughter-daughter. The water then drains back down through the Castle's caterpillars. Capertillers. Copillanies. Capilleeries. Capillaries. Every now and then, there's a big tank like this one."

He stopped talking, but didn't start swimming again. After a while, Tal said, "Uh, Uncle Ebbitt? Are we going somewhere?"

"Of course we're going *somewhere*," replied Ebbitt. "There's not much point rescuing you if we don't go *somewhere*."

"Can we go soon?" asked Tal. "I'm not much of a swimmer."

"Really?" said Ebbitt, looking surprised. "Neither am I. Does it matter?"

He stopped moving his arms, but didn't sink. Tal looked down and saw that the old man was standing on his Spiritshadow, who was gently paddling beneath him.

Tal's shadowguard was trying to do the same thing. Experimentally, Tal stopped paddling, but quickly started again when his head instantly sank beneath the surface. In its weakened condition his shadowguard didn't have the strength to keep him up.

Ebbitt started swimming again. They swam for what seemed like ages to Tal, before Ebbitt's Sunstone lit up the end of the corridor. Tal had expected to see a door or another hatch or some other obvious way out, but the corridor ended in a large chamber that was also half full of water. The three sides of the chamber were riddled with different-sized tunnel entrances, many of them well above water level.

Ebbitt pointed at one and said, "That's it. That's the one we want. Capillary 17824567834567 – or thereabouts. Smear this on your face and hands."

He handed Tal a jar. It still had the top on, so the boy had to tread water and undo it at the same time, resulting in several momentary disappearances underwater. The third time Tal went under, Ebbitt snatched the jar back and easily unscrewed the lid.

"No enterprise," said Ebbitt gloomily, as he gave it back.

Tal spat out some water angrily, not caring if he hit his great-uncle. Then he looked in the jar. Whatever it was smelled horrible and it was a sickly yellow. Knowing Ebbitt, it was also probably totally unnecessary.

"What is it?" asked Tal.

"Insect repellent," said Ebbitt.

Tal hesitated. Surely it wasn't that important to put on insect repellent. Not now, even if it did look sticky enough to stay on in water.

"The people who built the Castle thought of everything," Ebbitt said absently, as he pointed to each tunnel entrance and mumbled numbers. Tal continued to hesitate, till his great-uncle added, "They even made these quite fascinating water spiders, about so big, to put in the cooling system and eat up any bits of meat, bodies and so on that might get accidentally caught up in here. Keep it free of contamination. Pity the spiders don't eat this revolting weed as well."

Tal stared at Ebbitt for a second, then slowly started to smear the yellow goo on his face and neck. He still wasn't sure if Ebbitt was playing a practical joke, but since the old man had spread his arms as wide as they would go when he'd said "about so big," Tal didn't want to take any chances.

When Tal had finished, Ebbitt also applied the repellent. Tal could see traces of a previous application, so perhaps it wasn't a joke. Then they both climbed up to the tunnel – or capillary – that Ebbitt had pointed to.

It was even narrower than the heating tunnels, only wide enough to crawl through. Tal was relieved to see that it was almost dry, with the merest trickle of water in the middle. At least, he was relieved until Ebbitt mumbled something about the water spiders being called that because they could swim and dive as well as run around on dry land.

"We'll play Colours to see who goes first," announced Ebbitt, who was once again supported by his Spiritshadow. Tal, who was delicately balanced with his feet in one tunnel and his elbows on the next, groaned.

"I'll go first, or last, or whatever," he said. "Where does this tunnel go anyway?"

"Now, now, don't spoil my fun," said Ebbitt. "This capillary goes to an artery, a bigger tunnel. We'll go along that and then through another capillary, then down through a valve and then we'll come out right inside the Hall of Nightmares."

"Inside the Hall of Nightmares!"

"Of course." Ebbitt frowned. "Outside wouldn't be much use if we want to rescue your friend Milla, would it? Now let's play."

He held up his hand and the Sunstone ring there quickly shifted through the colours of the Seven Orders.

Tal groaned again and reached out his hand with its own Sunstone ring. His other hand clutched at the lip of the upper tunnel, while his shadowguard hung anxiously to his knees.

"Go," said Ebbitt. His ring flashed red as Tal's flashed violet. Colours was a children's game and often ended in stalemate. The object was to flash a Sunstone in a higher colour than your opponent. The catch was that you could use each colour only once in the entire game, and in the next round you couldn't use the next-highest or next-lowest colour to the one just played.

Tal won the first round, but could no longer use Violet at all or Indigo in the next round. Predictably, Ebbitt flashed Blue next, as did Tal. So it was still one-nil. Then Ebbitt flashed Violet, while Tal flashed Red. One-all. Then Tal flashed

Indigo and Ebbitt Orange. Two-one in favour of Tal. Ebbitt countered with Indigo, beating Tal's Green to make it two-all. Ebbitt finished with Green, and Tal was left with Orange, the final score three-two in Ebbitt's favour.

"I win," announced Ebbitt. "But you can go first."

"Thanks," said Tal nervously. He slid into the tunnel, trying not to listen as Ebbitt muttered something under his breath about water spiders.

# 22

Milla was lying in the crystal globe, saving her strength and pretending to be asleep, when she heard the sudden clang of metal hitting stone. She didn't react obviously, but her head moved slightly towards the sound and her eyes opened to narrow slits. Had her jailer returned and tripped over some of his own apparatus?

Whatever had happened, it was in one of the dark corners of the Hall. The globe was still brightly lit by beams of coloured light that continued to run through the silver wires. Everywhere else was dark.

Or was it? Milla watched a small light blossom

in the far corner – a surreptitious light that moved slowly towards her. Milla opened her eyes a little more, peering at it. She could see shapes round the light. And she could hear whispering as well. It sounded like the old man, Tal's great-uncle, whatever that meant. Milla had uncles, but not great ones.

"Probably have to carry her," he was saying. "Mind turned to jelly. Chance of recovery, mind you."

Milla kept silent. This could be a trick. But when she heard another whisper, she almost called out. It was Tal.

"She looks all right. Where's... who did you say... Fashnek?"

"Asleep, if we're lucky."

They came up to the globe. Milla kept still, though she was surprised to see that both were sodden and covered in little bits of dark muck that looked like the seaweed the Mother Crone had served them in the Ruin Ship.

Ebbitt cautiously moved the metal stands and their Sunstones, pointing their beams up to the ceiling. Tal touched the globe, then tapped on it near Milla's face. She sprang up and he jumped back.

"Milla!"

"Who else would I be?" asked Milla. But she smiled, clearly with some effort for it only lasted an instant.

"You're all right!" exclaimed Tal. "What happened?"

"The man who is half shadow tried to change my dreams," Milla said. "But I called the Crones and they came to my dream and scared him away."

"Really?" asked Ebbitt. "I'd like to meet one of these Crones. I never married, but anyone who could—"

"Not now, Uncle," said Tal firmly, noticing Milla's expression. "Where's Fashnek?"

"He left," replied Milla. "Can you release me? I have not found the trick of opening this prison."

"Sure," said Tal, but it proved easier said than done. The globe appeared to be solid crystal. Under bright light there were lots of tiny holes in the bottom of it, but they couldn't help get Milla out.

While Tal pored over the globe trying to find a switch, lever or something to open it, Ebbitt wandered about, looking at the Sunstones on their metal stands. The stands stood in grooved tracks on the floor so they could be accurately placed.

Several books were laid out on a table beyond the ring of Sunstones. Ebbitt flipped through them with interest, while his Spiritshadow stood guard near the door.

Finally, Tal had to admit that he couldn't find a way to open the globe. "I suppose we'll have to wait for Fashnek," he said. "I guess I can blind him and then we'll tie him up and make him open the globe."

Milla shook her head. "He has three shadows with him, as well as the one that grows from his flesh," she said. "You could not overcome them all."

"Three S-S-Spiritshadows!" stuttered Tal. "He can't!"

"He could," said Ebbitt. "No one ever sees Fashnek. Well, no one he doesn't want to see. I suppose he must see someone. Or someone must see him."

"Sushin," Tal declared. "He's the one behind everything. He's got a new Spiritshadow too. I just don't understand what he wants."

"I never understand," said Ebbitt. "Plots and

schemes, secret meetings. It's all too hard. What's the point of going Violet anyway?"

Tal shook his head, ignoring the old man. Sometimes he *really* didn't understand his great-uncle. Besides, whatever Sushin was up to, it wasn't anything as normal as trying to climb to a higher Order. He could do that the regular way, without putting people in pits and kidnapping children.

"By the way," Ebbitt added, "that book over there is very interesting. Did you know this globe was originally invented to help people with their dreams? Not to give them nightmares at all. The Castle builders were really very clever—"

"Did it tell you how to open the globe?" asked Tal crossly, before Ebbitt could blather on about what the globe used to be for.

"Naturally," Ebbitt replied. He raised his ring and sent a quick combination of coloured lights at the globe. As they hit, there was a ringing sound, like a tuning fork or a crystal glass being struck. The globe split in half like an oyster.

Milla jumped out and stretched. Then she clapped

her fists together to Ebbitt, showing thanks and respect. Tal waited for her to do it to him as well, but she didn't. Instead she immediately started looking for her Merwin-horn sword and armour.

"Where do we go now?" asked Tal nervously. "We'll have to hide somewhere. I'll need to put together some sort of disguise so I can go looking for the Codex and Gref."

"Mmmm," replied Ebbitt. He was momentarily intent on cleaning out his ear, which had suffered from an intrusion of the green weed. "I've been thinking about that, and thinking about my thinking, and then thinking about me thinking about my thinking—"

"And?" Tal interrupted.

"The Codex is probably in Aenir."

"Why?"

"Because there is no power in the Castle that could restrain the Codex if it wanted to be consulted," said Ebbitt. "But there is in Aenir. The Codex is almost alive, my boy. It was made to be read. If it was in the Castle it would have found a way for people to consult it. Therefore, it must be in Aenir. You'll have to bring it back."

"Right," said Tal slowly. "I can't believe this all started because I needed one Sunstone!"

"Is that when it started?" Ebbitt asked innocently. "I think you'll find that, whatever it is, it started long ago. Sushin is not the only one with secret business and strange ways. Your father is not the only Chosen who is missing, nor is Gref the only child. I should have looked into matters long ago, but I missed my chance. I think it is long past time someone did what I didn't and brought the Codex back and set all to rights. You seem to be just the right person for the job."

Tal looked at Ebbitt. For once the old man seemed quite serious. He wasn't smiling dreamily, or cleaning his ear, or staring at something no one else could see.

"Well, there's one thing I can do right now," Tal said. "And that is to get Milla a Sunstone."

He reached out to grab the one closest to him, one that was set in a clawed hand atop a silver stand. But before his fingers closed on it, Ebbitt grabbed him and twisted his arm away.

"Not one of those!" said Ebbitt. "They're full of

nightmares, full of evil dreams. No use to a charming young Icecarl."

Milla snorted, though Tal wasn't sure if this was because of the nightmare-filled Sunstone or because Ebbitt had called her charming. She'd found her charred armour and put it back on. She had also reclaimed her Merwin-horn sword.

"I have seen enough of your Castle and enough of its shadows," she announced. "Give me the Sunstone, Tal, so I may return to the clean Ice."

Tal looked at the ring. He could understand why Milla wanted to take it and go, but he still needed it.

"What about the thirteen sleeps?"

"Twelve now," said Milla sternly. "I will wait if I must. But I am asking you now as a friend of the clan, Tal. The clan whose blood you share."

Tal looked at the ring again, then at Milla. He did feel that he owed her something. It was his fault she'd got captured and been taken here, to the Hall of Nightmares. She was also clearly at risk in the Castle. Perhaps he should give her the Sunstone. It might even be easier for him to not have to worry about Milla...

"I can't give it to you," Tal finally said. "Not yet."

He met Milla's gaze, but saw no sign there of what she would do. Surely she wouldn't try to take the stone by force?

His shadowguard felt his tension and stood up beside him, stretching into the shape of a small Borzog. Ebbitt's Spiritshadow watched from the door, but rose up on all four legs and tensed to spring.

"What's all this fuss?" asked Ebbitt. "Give me that Sunstone, Tal."

"This is my business, Uncle," Tal snapped. It was the first time he had ever spoken in such a way to a full, adult Chosen. If he had done it in public, he would have earned deluminents from everyone around.

"Give it to me," Ebbitt repeated. He held out his bony hand. His Spiritshadow padded over and stood next to Tal, and tilted its head to look at him.

"Whose side are you on?" Tal asked. He took off the ring and angrily put it in Ebbitt's hand. Tears of rage were forming in his eyes, but there was nothing he could do. If Ebbitt wanted to take the Sunstone and give it to Milla, Tal would just have to put up with it. He could climb another Tower, the Orange one, and do a better job of stealing one. He would steal half a dozen Sunstones!

Ebbitt didn't hand the Sunstone to Milla. He held it up to his eye and flashed a rainbow of light at it from his own Sunstone. Then he threw it up in the air and a sharp white beam lanced out at it from the ring on his right hand. There was a spray of sparks and the old man caught the ring again.

Tal blinked, and then he saw that Ebbitt was holding two rings now. The old one had been perfectly sliced in half.

So had the Sunstone.

"One each," said Ebbitt, handing Tal and Milla smaller but still perfectly functioning Sunstones, judging from the glow in the depths of each stone.

"Is it strong enough to be a Primary?" asked Tal as he slid the thinner ring on his finger. He'd had no idea that Sunstones could be split.

"Easily," said Ebbitt, sniffing. "That's a strong stone. One of the originals, I'd say. Not one of these modern imitations, with hardly ten years' sunlight in them. That's a three- or four-century stone. Besides, it was two stones to start with. Someone put them together long ago, when frogs still had legs."

"You can put Sunstones together?" asked Tal.

Why hadn't he been taught any of this Sunstone lore? He would be finished at the Lectorium in a month and he knew there were no more classes on Sunstones. Perhaps the lectors didn't know themselves?

Ebbitt was an eccentric, but Tal had always known he was a very learned one. He hadn't suspected that this learning would include the secret ways of the Castle, the nature of Sunstones, or anything like that.

"The Far Raiders thank you," said Milla. This time, she did knock her knuckles together for Tal as well as Ebbitt. "Now, how do I return to the heating tunnels?"

"Tricky," said Ebbitt. "They'll be looking for Tal now and for you soon, Milla. What with Spiritshadows searching you out it could be very hard to get back down."

"Searching us out?" asked Milla. "How? Like a Wrack Hound, by smell?"

"Wrack Hounds?" asked Ebbitt, brightening. "What might they be—"

"Spiritshadows, searching," interrupted Tal, to hasten the old man along. He glanced nervously at the door.

"Oh, yes," agreed Ebbitt. "Any of the Spiritshadows that have touched you will remember the feel of your essence. They can sense that from quite a long way away. Very clever. I've had mine do it to track down friends. I wouldn't be surprised if they're already on their way."

"Well, let's not wait for them!" urged Tal.

Ebbitt let out a sigh and looked back at the apparatus and the books. Tal steered him back to the capillary tunnel. Tal and Milla bombarded him with questions as they helped the old man up into the ceiling.

"What do you mean, they sense us?"

"How far can they do this sensing?"

"Can anything stop them from sensing us?"

After Ebbitt was safely up in the capillary tunnel, Tal suddenly stopped asking questions and said, "Ebbitt! The insect repellent! For Milla!"

Milla didn't ask what the yellow muck was. But she smeared it on immediately. She had just finished her face when the door to the Hall of Nightmares suddenly opened, letting in a rush of light.

Fashnek stood there, his Spiritshadow behind him and two other Spiritshadows at his side. He gaped at the open globe then saw Milla leaping up into what he thought was a solid ceiling.

"Seize her!" he roared. But he stepped back himself. He had been frightened by Milla and the Crones in her dream. Now she had escaped from the crystal globe without a Sunstone! She was clearly an even more dangerous and powerful an enemy than he'd thought.

Ebbitt sealed the hatch behind them, then put his Sunstone down the front of his shirt. It was followed by his Spiritshadow, which shrank down and curled round it. Tal and his shadowguard did the same thing. Milla's stone still shone from her pocket until Tal dimmed it for her. In total darkness they would be safe from the pursuing Spiritshadows, who needed light to be able to do anything.

"Hold my leg," whispered Ebbitt. "Milla, hold Tal's."

Clutching on to one another, they began to crawl. Tal had to fight the urge to get his Sunstone out. It was just like the Veil, when he'd passed through it. The darkness seemed to press on him physically and he found it hard to breathe. It got worse and worse until he was panting very quickly and clutching Ebbitt's foot so hard that the old man yelped in pain.

Tal was even more afraid because he wasn't sure that Ebbitt knew where he was going. They could be crawling anywhere – to the lair of the water spiders – thousands of them, boiling over, a great pit of water spiders, which would find that square of skin that Tal had missed putting repellent on and their fangs would—

There was something on Tal's leg. It had to be a water spider. It had to be! Or maybe it was Milla, holding on. He wanted to kick at it and roll over, but maybe it was Milla and he couldn't breathe and—

Ebbitt stopped.

"We should be far enough away," he whispered. "I'm going to try a little light."

Tal almost sobbed with relief, but he couldn't help himself craning his head back to be ready when the light came. Though he had no idea what he'd do if he looked back and found himself staring into the multifaceted eyes and piercing fangs of a water spider...

The light came. There was only Milla, holding on to Tal's leg. There were no water spiders.

Tal's expression must have given him away, because Milla quickly ran her fingers across Tal's knee, like a spider. He flinched and Milla laughed. It was only the second time Tal had heard Milla laugh.

"There was a spider," said Milla. "It had eyes like ice crystals, but with a light inside, not a reflection. It waved its legs at me, but did not move."

"Where?" croaked Tal, his throat suddenly very, very dry.

"Back in the cross-tunnel," said Milla, pointing at an intersection that was far too close for Tal's liking. "But there was nothing to fear. I would have slain it if it approached."

"They are hard to kill," warned Ebbitt. "We had best get on before the repellent wears off."

"Where?" asked Milla.

Tal looked back at Ebbitt. The old man shrugged and smiled. The dreamy smile.

"If the Spiritshadows can sense us," Tal said, "it's going to be hard to hide anywhere and almost impossible to get you down to the Underfolk levels. Even if we could make it there, I don't know where Crow and his friends found us."

"I'd find it," said Milla. "But I believe you. If we cannot go there yet, where can we go?"

"We have to let the Empress know that Sushin

is doing things illegally in her name and with her guards," said Tal. "Once she knows, she'll put everything right."

He hesitated then added, "But I probably wouldn't be able to get to the Empress either. Unless these capillaries go up to Violet?"

"They do," replied Ebbitt. "But they get ever so narrow and ever so small, almost like they're not there at all."

"But Milla might be able to use them to get down further, down to the Underfolk levels," said Tal.

"No, no, no." Ebbitt shook his head. "The water spiders spin their webs below Red Seven. All part of the plan, you see, to catch what shouldn't get past. We were once so very clever."

"Can't go up, can't go down, can't see my mother, can't go anywhere normal," said Tal as he counted each possibility on his fingers. Then he made a fist and struck it into the palm of his other hand. "There must be *somewhere* we can go!"

"Aenir," said Ebbitt. "I told you. It's almost time for you to get a Spiritshadow anyway, and you, we, *everyone* needs the Codex. The Spiritshadows won't be able to sniff you out here if you're there."

Tal thought about this for a good minute.

"It's forbidden to go to Aenir before the Day of Ascension," he pointed out.

"That's only because it's safer when all the Chosen are there together," said Ebbitt. "And it wasn't always forbidden. I've been over by myself. Several times."

Tal thought about that a bit longer. He didn't seem to have a lot of choice.

"If we go, what will happen to our bodies?" he asked finally. "We couldn't leave them here. We might be gone for weeks."

"What is Aenir?" asked Milla suddenly. "Why would we leave our bodies?"

"Aenir is the spirit world," Tal explained shortly. "It is another land, which the Chosen can enter. We leave our bodies here and our spirits go there."

"Ah, like a dream," said Milla.

"No," said Tal. "It is real, but different. If you have the strength and a powerful Sunstone, you can take things there – and bring them back. It is a place of magic. The seeds that Sunstones grow from come from Aenir. So do Spiritshadows."

"The source of Shadow," Milla whispered. "Perhaps I should see this, to report to the Crones."

"We can't go unless our bodies are safe," said Tal. "So it's pointless thinking about it."

"The Mausoleum," said Ebbitt suddenly. "A good place for bodies. Dead or alive!"

The Mausoleum was where Chosen were finally laid to rest. It was rare for a Chosen to die young because their lives could usually be prolonged by Sunstones, but there were always accidents, or those who had grown weary of life, or who made mistakes with the healing power of their stones.

The Mausoleum occupied the second-biggest chamber in the Castle, in the neutral levels on the southern side. It had a domed ceiling, cut from the rock and adorned with thousands of Sunstone chips to give the impression of stars. Unlike the rest of the Castle, it was not lit by anything brighter. The Mausoleum lay in perpetual twilight, under a night sky as it might be seen above the Veil.

Every single Chosen whose remains rested there occupied a lavishly decorated stone coffin, surmounted by a statue of their Spiritshadow. The vast hall was lined with row after row of fantastic statues, Spiritshadows carved in white-and-red marble, in greenstone, or in black, gold-shot granite. Many were adorned with gold and silver, or set with dull, ordinary gems like diamonds and rubies.

No capillaries of the cooling system entered the Mausoleum, so Ebbitt led them out nearby. They sneaked through the Preparing Room, which was fortunately empty of Chosen, dead or alive.

Instead of going through the huge metal gates that were covered with the names of the dead Chosen, Ebbitt pointed them through a nondescript door, into the Underfolk stonemasons' workshop.

An Underfolk sculptor working there looked at them, but Ebbitt made a sign with his hand, and the woman turned back to her steady chipping at a block of yellow-green stone. Underfolk did all the basic preparation of the statues, which were then finished by Chosen artists, who used Light rather than clumsy metal tools, not to mention their supposedly superior talents.

"Now all you have to do is find two very old coffins," whispered Ebbitt as they left the workshop and entered the Mausoleum proper, again through an unobtrusive door.

"What?" Tal whispered back. Somehow it didn't seem polite to speak normally in the Mausoleum, though there didn't appear to be anyone around to hear them. Milla kept scanning the rows, her eyes moving slowly from side to side, checking to see if anything moved.

"The north corner," suggested Ebbitt, leading the way down an aisle of coffins and statues. "The oldest. Nothing but dust inside. Not too icky. Scoop it out and settle in."

"You let bodies rot inside these stone boxes?" asked Milla with a shudder. It was the first time Tal had seen her show visible signs of disgust. "Aren't there any animals that could eat them?"

"It's just the way we do things here," said Tal. "It's different, that's all."

"Savages," Milla muttered under her breath. She longed to be out on the clean Ice again, with the cold wind blowing. It was too hot in the Castle, and too enclosed. There were always walls, even in the very big rooms like this one.

"I guess if we're going to do it, we'd better get on with it," said Tal as they came to coffins that were obviously older than the others they'd seen. The style of carved decorations was quite different from those to the south, and the stone was more worn.

Though the decorations were individual, the stone coffins all had the same basic design. The statue on top could be pushed and the lid would swivel to reveal an opening.

Tal and Milla had to try a couple before they found a statue that would move. It rumbled aside, and Tal hesitantly looked in while Milla stood by disapprovingly. There was nothing inside but what looked like a layer of old, old earth.

"Ebbitt, can you help Milla cross into Aenir before you go yourself?" asked Tal. "I think I can remember how... how Dad did it last Ascension."

"Hmmm?" Ebbitt had been staring at a particular statue, remembering the Spiritshadow and its master. They had been friends long ago and his death was still an unexplained mystery. Ebbitt was only now realising that this applied to many of his old, departed friends.

"Help Milla? Of course. But I'm not going with you."

"What? You have to!" Tal insisted. "I've only been to Aenir with everyone else! Without you—"

"I need to stay here," mumbled Ebbitt. "Someone will have to keep watch over your bodies. Even if they are hidden in the coffins."

"I'm not sure this is the best thing to do then," said Tal, who was having serious second thoughts. "Maybe I should try to see the Empress first. Surely she would listen—"

Ebbitt shook his head. "The Empress sees no one she does not summon. Sushin and whoever he is in league with control the Imperial Guards and that means they control access to Her Majesty. Find the Codex and it will lead us to Gref, and perhaps more. The Codex knows much that is hidden. I think also that you must try to get the most powerful Spiritshadow you can, Tal. You will need its help in the days ahead."

Milla looked at Ebbitt and said bluntly, "Tal was wrong. You are not a crazy old man."

"I never said crazy," protested Tal. "I said *not exactly normal.*"

"Crazy is more accurate," replied Ebbitt. "But there are different kinds of crazy."

"Can you try to see my mother?" asked Tal anxiously. "And make sure she is looked after until I can come back and get her? And Kusi too?"

Ebbitt nodded, and his Spiritshadow bowed its great maned head.

"I will be back, with a Spiritshadow and the Codex," Tal vowed. "And we'll find Gref and my father, and heal Mother, and we'll see the Empress and get Sushin dimmed and..."

Tal's voice trailed off as he saw Ebbitt's expression. He had the look of someone who wanted to believe in something, but couldn't.

# 25

Tal climbed into the coffin and stretched out. It was cold and dark, but surprisingly comfortable. He took the Sunstone ring off his finger and held it with the thumb and forefinger of both hands, resting it on his chest.

His shadowguard slipped over the side of the coffin and then slid in under him. Tal was surprised for a moment, then he realised that it wanted to go home to Aenir. He had turned thirteen and three-quarters and it was time for Tal to release it, and bind a Spiritshadow instead.

He took a few deep breaths, closed his eyes and began to mentally recite the Way to Aenir.

As the words – which he had learned by rote without understanding their meaning – rolled through his mind, red light began to spill out of his Sunstone, flowing like water across his chest and down his stomach.

Tal could feel the light spreading, but he continued his silent recitation. The red light flowed over his face and over his feet. Then orange light welled out of the Sunstone and slowly covered him, swirling through the red.

More colours followed until all seven had flowed out and mingled. Milla watched in fascination as Tal was covered in an iridescent rainbow cocoon that glowed and shimmered. His face could only be glimpsed through the shroud of many colours, but Milla noted that he didn't move at all. Even his chest had ceased the rise and fall of breath.

"He has gone to Aenir," said Ebbitt with satisfaction. He pushed at the statue and the coffin lid slid back. In a second, it was just another Chosen tomb, with no sign of the hibernating boy inside.

"Now I go," said Milla. "But I do not know how."

They selected another coffin, one adorned with a Spiritshadow statue in a shape that vaguely reminded Milla of a Merwin. It had a single, long horn sprouting from its forehead, though otherwise it was more like a broad-shouldered, long-armed human. Its legs were a bit like a Wreska's, with toed hooves.

Milla settled into the coffin and held her Sunstone as Tal had done. She laid her sword under her elbow. She hoped it would go with her to this Spirit World. She hoped that the Crones would also be able to find her there, in case she dreamed. But that seemed unlikely. She had never heard them speak of Aenir.

"I will speak the Way to Aenir and you must repeat it silently inside your head," said Ebbitt. "You must also concentrate on each of the seven colours at the right time. I will throw a ray from my own Sunstone to show you. Do you understand?"

"Yes," said Milla. This was another adventure worthy of Ulla Strong-Arm. These Chosen – especially the ones conspiring against Tal – were very dangerous and powerful. The more she learned of their secrets, the better. She would return to the Ruin Ship not only with a Sunstone, but knowledge for the good of all the clans.

Ebbitt began to speak and Milla concentrated on his words.

Colour spread across her, but she kept her eyes open, watching for Ebbitt's colour changes. She could feel the colours change in the Sunstone and each colour produced a different sensation on her skin.

It wasn't at all like going to sleep and falling into a dream, as she thought it might be. As each colour passed her eyes it changed the world a little. Ebbitt's face faded and so did his Spiritshadow. They became patterns and then blurs of light. Everything became a rainbow, so bright that Milla couldn't help blinking.

Then the colours started to separate again and she saw other patterns. Her skin felt hot and cold at the same time, in different patches. Her toes tingled and she felt as if she were falling, suddenly dizzy.

She could no longer hear Ebbitt's voice. For a moment she felt a stab of fear, as if without his words she might be lost between the two worlds.

Then the patches of colour became sharper and sharper, solidifying into a bright blue band that filled the upper part of her vision. The light dimmed a little, but was still bright.

Milla closed her eyes. Sound suddenly hit her – a musical, happy sound, like a bone pipe played in trills.

Wind blew across her face. Milla opened her eyes. She stood upright on something soft and springy that looked a bit like long ice lichen. There were tall plants near her, larger than anything she had ever seen. Small coloured animals with wings flew among the plants, making the whistling noises.

It was bright. There was a huge light in the sky, a hot, fierce light. Milla started to look up at it, but Tal was suddenly there, shielding her face with his hand.

"Don't look," he said. "That's the sun."

Milla looked at Tal instead. She recognised him, but he looked different. He was shorter and slighter, and his skin glowed with a soft lustre. The Sunstone ring on his finger caught the light and surrounded his hand with tiny rainbows.

She looked at her own hands and saw that they glowed too, and her fingers seemed longer.

"Am I me?" she asked in wonder.

"You are what you are here," said Tal. "Aenir is a realm of spirit and magic, and we are part of it now, less solid. Try to jump."

He jumped himself and went soaring up to grab a branch, easily three or four times as high as Milla. Then he moved back down, falling slowly, like a feather.

Milla flexed her knees and saw her sword lying on the ground. She picked it up, stroking the soft, long lichen on the way.

"Grass," said Tal, seeing her puzzled look. "It's good to lie on in the sun."

Milla put the sword through her belt and took a practice leap. That carried her almost into one of the big plants.

"Watch out for the trees!" laughed Tal.

"Trees," repeated Milla wonderingly. "We have a story about trees, before the Veil was made and the Ice came. I didn't think they were like this."

"This is a forest," said Tal. "Lots of trees together."

"It is good," said Milla, sniffing the wind. There was no scent of cold stone here. The only troubling thing was the light, but that was just habit. Her eyes must have changed with everything else, because she felt no need to squint.

"The only thing is," Tal said, "we should have come out at where we normally do, on the Chosen Plain. It's one of the few places that always stays the same, we have houses and stores and so on there."

"We can walk there," said Milla, unconcerned.

"But I don't know where it is," Tal confessed. "I'm lost."

Instinctively, Tal looked for his shadowguard, to
ask it where the Chosen Enclave was. Once he
knew that, he would be able to work out where
they should go.

But as Tal turned, his shadow moved with him.
Just like a natural shadow. Too much like a natural
shadow in fact. The shadowguard had never been
that good at mimicking an ordinary shadow.

Tal bent down to touch it and felt grass rather
than the cool touch of Shadowflesh.

"It's gone," he said numbly. "I've got my natural
shadow back."

"Good," said Milla. She was looking round, nose

wrinkling. Something had disturbed her, though she couldn't quite work out what it was.

"You don't understand," said Tal, shaking his head in disbelief and sorrow. "It's been with me all my life. I knew it would go when it was time for me to get a Spiritshadow, but I thought it would wait till I was ready to let it go! It could have at least said goodbye…"

Something hissed from behind one of the trees. The warning hiss of the shadowguard. Then a small, furry, but somehow recognisable animal sprang out, jumped up on Tal's chest, licked him across the face and then jumped away again.

Milla had her knife in her hand, ready to throw, but she hesitated. Before she could change her mind, whatever it was disappeared at high speed through the trees.

"Was that it?" she asked hesitantly. "No longer shadow?"

"They're not shadows in Aenir, not until we bind them and take them back," replied Tal, wiping his face and his eyes with his sleeve. "I guess… I guess it always liked being a Dattu because it was one here."

He shook his head a few times, as if to clear it, then looked down at his natural shadow again. He felt very alone without his shadowguard. It had saved him countless times – from danger and embarrassment and difficulty. Now all he had was a useless shadow.

An *almost* useless shadow, he corrected himself, because he would use it as part of a trap to catch some creature of Aenir and turn it into a Spiritshadow to take back to the Castle.

Milla was still poised in the clearing between the trees, a troubled look on her face.

"Something is happening," she said. "Listen!"

Tal stood still and listened. At first, all he could hear was the wind in the branches above him. Then he heard it too. Distant thunder, which was slowly growing closer.

"Thunder," he said. "That means lightning too."

"Lightning?" Milla asked. "What is that?"

"Um, hard to explain," said Tal. He'd only seen it in Aenir, for lightning did not pass through the Veil on the Dark World. But it did strike the towers and he had often heard the thunder that accompanied lightning, even inside the Castle. The lectors had also given several lessons about lightning and how it could be mimicked with Light magic.

The Icecarls would hear thunder too, but they wouldn't know of its connection with lightning, because they would never see it. "Lightning is kind of concentrated light that comes down from the sky. You can work out how far away the lightning is by counting the time between the flash and the sound of the thunder."

"I can't see any flash," said Milla. "There are too many trees—"

She stopped in midsentence, because off in the distance a tree was slowly moving. Not just swaying from side to side, but actually walking.

Tal and Milla jumped at the same time, as a ripple spread through the grass under their feet. The closest tree shivered and somehow stretched a little taller. One of its exposed roots flexed and then pulled out of the ground with a popping sound.

"The trees, they walk?" asked Milla. She seemed more pleased at the notion than afraid.

"Not usually," replied Tal suspiciously, stepping back. "Though in Aenir, who knows?"

All the trees around them were uprooting themselves. They swayed and rolled, but somehow didn't fall. Tal and Milla backed away from the closest one, even though it made no threatening movements. When enough of its root system was clear, all the roots wriggled like thousands of tiny legs and the tree started slowly moving away from them.

All the trees were walking. They were heading off in every direction except towards the storm. Walking away from the sound of thunder, which was getting closer with every passing moment.

"The trees are fleeing," said Milla. "From the thunder?"

"Maybe," said Tal. The forest had cleared out behind them, as trees shook and swayed, shedding leaves and branches in their haste to depart. "Sometimes things happen in Aenir for no reason."

Milla snorted, a sound that Tal knew meant she didn't think much of his local knowledge. He continued to look out at the sky, trying to remember everything he'd been taught about storms in Aenir. Dim memories of the Lectorium came into his head, mostly of Lector Norval droning on.

All he could remember was a story about Storm Shepherds, strange creatures that looked like human-shaped clouds, ten or twelve stretches tall, which were thought to be harmless if left alone. This didn't seem very useful.

Neither did Tal's memories of previous visits to Aenir with his family. They had always stayed close to the Chosen Enclave, though his father had travelled further afield.

The trees continued to move away and before long Tal and Milla could see a continuous line of dark clouds on the horizon. Flashes of lightning also became visible, forking down from the black sky. Tal looked at Milla and saw her staring at the lightning, totally entranced. Then she shook her head and said, "It is not dishonourable to seek shelter from a storm. We should follow the trees."

"I'm not sure," replied Tal nervously. He looked at the rapidly retreating forest heading towards what he thought was probably south, then at the low line of barren, rocky hills to the east and west, and then at the clouds again. "Maybe we should go that way."

He pointed at the closer hills.

"Why?" asked Milla.

Tal gulped and said, "Because I think that storm is going to turn this whole place into a lake."

"A what?" asked Milla.

"Look at the darkness under the clouds!" Tal said urgently. "Look around! We're in a basin and the clouds are dumping rain. This whole area's going to fill up. It's going to flood, turn into a lake. A small sea!"

Milla needed no further explanation. She took one calculating look at the encroaching clouds and then started to run to the closest hill. Tal was right behind her.

# 27

They were barely halfway to the hill when Tal had to stop to regain his breath. Milla stopped too. Even though she wasn't breathing hard, Tal noticed she held two fingers to her side, where she'd been wounded by the Merwin. It must be hurting.

Tal looked back at the storm front and saw that not only was it much closer, it had already dumped so much rain that a small flood was running ahead of the clouds. Muddy water was rushing over the ground where the forest had stood, eddying into the tree root holes before flowing ever onwards.

The thunder and lightning were fading, much to Tal's relief. Though it was probably only because the clouds were so full of rain. So the chance of being struck by lightning had decreased, but they were still in imminent danger of drowning.

"We'll make it," said Milla, as they started to run again. There was water under their feet now and the first raindrops were falling all around them. But the hill was close.

They made it with a few minutes to spare. Panting, they watched the front of the floodwater strike the high ground and be turned back in a flurry of ripples. The hill wasn't very large, only a hundred or so stretches tall, but Tal hoped the water would not rise that high.

"It is strange," said Milla, holding out her palm to catch several heavy raindrops that splashed off her fingers. "Like snow, but warmer and... more free."

"Not that much warmer," grumbled Tal. "We'd better find some shelter."

The hillside was rapidly turning into mud, but they managed to clamber up to the crest. Tal stopped to look back down, but Milla started down the other side.

Tal couldn't see very far because of the rain, but

where the forest had been was now just a swirling mass of dirty water. If he hadn't seen the trees there before, he would never have believed it wasn't a muddy lake.

"Tal!"

Tal looked away and hurried down after Milla. She sounded like she'd found shelter.

She had. She was standing outside the mouth of a cave, with her Merwin-horn sword in her hand, holding it up so its light shone in the entrance.

Something reflected back, something red and shiny, deep inside. Tal saw it and instantly an image flashed into his head. A Beastmaker card, with two red eyes that were not eyes shining in a cave entrance.

The Cavernmouth card.

"Milla! Trap!" he screamed, thrusting out his hand with the Sunstone ring, thoughts focusing on its power.

Milla reacted instantly to his warning, throwing herself to one side. She felt the rush of air but didn't see the two enormous jaws that shot out from the cave – long jaws of dark bone and still darker teeth – hundreds and hundreds of teeth, crooked and shambling, like helter-skelter rows of thorns.

The jaws closed with a clash, exactly where Milla had been standing a split second before. As they opened again for another snatch, Tal sent a wide spray of white-hot sparks straight down the open gullet of the beast.

A hideous bellow echoed from inside the hill and the jaws snapped back inside. Then the whole Cavernmouth retreated deeper into its burrow, dragging earth and stone down behind it as a last-ditch defence.

Tal lowered his hand, his whole arm shaking. The Sunstone on his finger still shone brightly, small sparks fizzing out to blacken his knuckles. Tal looked at the stone and brought it back under control.

Milla had crawled away, circling back up and round the crest, ready to counterattack. She came down the hill and looked at the pile of raw earth where the Cavernmouth's decoy hole had been.

"What was that?" she asked. Tal didn't notice that she had to moisten her mouth before she could speak.

"Cavernmouth," said Tal. "All jaws and stomach. I should have told you about them before."

Milla shrugged. "I did not tell you about everything that lives on the Ice. But I will be more careful. I must live to bring a Sunstone back to the Far Raiders."

"Well, we need to find the Codex before we can go back," Tal muttered. He raised his arm and watched the water run off it. "Though finding somewhere dry would do for now."

Milla gazed into the distance, then shook her head in disbelief. "You can see so far here! But the forest is already out of sight, and look! That hill is moving, too, like a dying Selski of earth and stone. I know it is not a dream and yet I doubt my senses. It is too light. Soon it will be dark, like home. The sun is falling down."

She pointed at the red light that was spreading over the hills. Sure enough, the sun was beginning to set.

"It'll come up again," said Tal, as much to reassure himself as anything. "I guess we'll have to camp here somehow."

It wasn't an attractive option. They only had their dirty, dishevelled furs and Milla's stinking armour. No sleeping furs, or cooking stove, or anything. Just a muddy hillside and continuous, beating rain.

They sat down together and glumly looked down on the rising waters of the new lake. It was still filling up, or flowing elsewhere, because there was quite a strong current heading south, carrying all the debris left by the fleeing forest.

Tal looked at one particularly large leaf floating past. It had curled up in the middle and its stalk was like the prow of a proud ship. That started him thinking. If only they had a ship themselves, or at least a raft, they could let the current take them somewhere. Anywhere had to be better than this.

But they didn't have anything to make a raft with.

Except light, Tal suddenly thought. He could use the solid light spell, the one he'd learned in order to make the stairway leading out of the pit. If he could make a stairway, he could make a raft. With two of them to concentrate on it, it would be easier to maintain as well.

"We can make a boat!" he exclaimed, jumping up. "A boat of light."

Then he sighed and sat down again, even as Milla got up.

"I forgot you aren't a Chosen," he said. "I wouldn't be able to keep it going by myself, and you don't know how to use your Sunstone properly."

"Teach me," Milla said. It almost came out as an order, but there was a faint question there too, a hopefulness that Tal wouldn't have noticed if he hadn't spent so much time with Milla.

Tal looked up at her. Could he teach her? The basics of concentration and reinforcement weren't that hard. He would make the boat, and Milla would only need to concentrate on colour and intensity to reinforce his Sunstone with her own.

But *should* he teach her? She was an Icecarl. Maybe an enemy. He still thought she might try to kill him once she was free of the Crone's Quest. She might regret killing him, but she'd do it because she'd said she would.

If Tal taught her Light magic, he'd be handing her a weapon.

On the other hand, there were plenty more dangers in Aenir, and he might be the one who needed help next time.

"All right," he said finally. "I'll teach you about Sunstones. What you need to know anyway."

"And I will teach you to fight," replied Milla.

She held out her hand and turned her wrist up, pushing back her wet and now even worse-smelling Selski-hide armour. Before Tal could groan, she'd reopened the triple cuts on her wrist.

The rain washed the blood away almost instantly, but Milla clenched her fist and waited till Tal hesitantly held out his wrist.

Milla cut as swiftly as the Crone and just as accurately. Tal flinched as the barest point of her knife cut the skin, imagining as always something worse. He didn't understand why the Icecarls cut at the wrist. Why not just prick their fingers with a flame-sterilised pin?

"Blood of the clan and bone of the ship," chanted Milla, wiping her wrist across Tal's, then placing the flat of the bone knife against both of them. She looked fiercely at Tal, till he repeated the words.

"Master and Student under the Sunstone," she continued, then she reversed the bone knife, still holding it between their wrists. "Student and Master under the Sword. By blood of the clan and bone of the ship. This we swear, with blood to the wind—"

She flicked both their wrists out, sending blood flying, though there was very little wind to take it.

"And blood to the—"

She hesitated and looked around, for here she would normally have said "Ice."

"Rain," said Tal, turning his wrist up to the sky. "Blood to the rain."

"Blood to the rain," confirmed Milla, following his gesture.

Two perfect, tear-shaped raindrops fell then, splashing on their cuts, completely removing the last traces of blood. No more welled up, as if the raindrops had miraculously healed the skin.

Tal and Milla stared down at their wrists then looked up at the sky, blinking through further rain. Both jumped as thunder suddenly crashed above them, sending a shock through the air.

They continued to stare up in amazement as

dark clouds shifted and roiled, and two clumps suddenly rolled down and out of the mass. Two vaguely man-shaped creatures of billowing black and grey formed out of the clumps. Their heads came first, then their arms grew out and then their legs stretched down to the hilltop.

Small streaks of lightning played backwards and forwards in their eyes, which were the only patches of white on the cloud creatures.

Milla and Tal backed away from the towering figures, which were easily three times their height.

One of the creatures loomed forward and roared, "Who gives blood to the rain at sunfall on old Hrigga Hill?"

Then the second one bellowed, "Who calls the Storm Shepherds?"

Then both shouted, the thunder of their voices knocking Tal and Milla to the ground.

"Who pays the blood price?"

Tal stared up at the huge figures, his mind racing. The blood price. In Aenir that meant a life. But he could trick them with his shadow and use it to bind one of them to him as a Spiritshadow. A

Storm Shepherd would be a great ally here and a very powerful Spiritshadow back in the Castle. But if he got any of the ritual wrong, his natural shadow would be lost and with it any chance of getting a Spiritshadow.

Should he take this chance, on the spur of the moment? Would there ever be a better opportunity? And what about Milla? There were two Storm Shepherds. The other one would demand her shadow as well and Milla wouldn't give it up. He would have to make her...

Tal darted a look at her. Their eyes met. He saw trust there. Milla expected him to fight at her side, not to try to sell her shadow.

Milla saw Tal's eyes flicker and his right hand rose with its Sunstone ring. Suddenly she knew that some betrayal lurked there. For all their blood pacts, he was not an Icecarl. She could not predict what he would do, or count on it being the best for clan and ship. An anger grew in her and she felt the Merwin-horn sword rise in her hand. She could hit him with the flat of the blade and then run—

Tal saw Milla's eyes grow hard, saw the sword rise.

He had to decide. Try and trick one Storm Shepherd with his shadow, and hope the other one would be able to take Milla's shadow too?

The Storm Shepherds roared.

Chosen boy and Icecarl girl faced each other. Their gaze was locked. Both knew that their fragile alliance was on the verge of breaking forever. Whoever looked away, whoever moved first, everything that came from it would be their fault.

Seconds passed and still neither moved. The Storm Shepherds raged. Lightning flashed and thunder crashed around the hilltop.

A thousand moments flashed through Tal's mind. His first encounter with Milla in the snow. Climbing the mast of the iceship. Crossing the Living Sea of Selski. The feeling of relief as he saw Milla stabbing the Merwin through the eye. The jump across the chasm. The heatway tunnels. The crystal globe with Milla waiting patiently inside it, when a Chosen would be a gibbering wreck.

All this was clearer to him, easier to remember than his life in the Castle before he fell.

Memories rushed through Milla's mind too. Tal

helping her up in front of the Selski. Blinding the Merwin. His hand under her head when she lay dying, the Merwin horn shining behind him. The jump across the chasm. How he'd looked covered in green weed, when he'd dropped into the Hall of Nightmares.

He wasn't an Icecarl, but he had never failed her, not when it really mattered. If a saga was ever sung of Milla Merwin-Slayer, she realised, it would have a potential Sword Thane in it as well as a would-be Shield Maiden.

Milla lowered her sword. At exactly the same time Tal let his hand drop back to his side.

Milla tilted her head. Tal nodded.

Together, they turned to face the blustering Storm Shepherds.

"I am Milla of the Far Raiders!" called out Milla.

"I am Tal of the Chosen," announced Tal.

Together they shouted, "We shall pay no price!"

Coming soon, book three of

# THE SEVENTH TOWER
## AENIR

Turn over for a sneak preview...

Tal climbed over the fallen door and through the doorway.

The room beyond had walls of stone and light, both holding back sand judging from the piles that had oozed through gaps where the magic barriers intersected with the stone.

In the middle of the room a boy sat cross-legged staring at Tal. A boy not much older than Tal, dressed in white trousers and a white shirt with blue cuffs. A Chosen boy.

Tal even knew who it was: Lenan of the Blue. He had disappeared last year. Every Day of Ascension all the Chosen children who had come of age would go forth to seek a Spiritshadow to bind. Not all of them came back.

But what was Lenan doing here? And where was Hazror?

"Greetings, Chosen," said Lenan. His voice sounded a little strange. Too high-pitched.

Tal had started to walk forwards to greet Lenan properly, but when he heard the voice he stopped.

The voice wasn't the only thing that was strange. Lenan was wearing several Sunstones round his neck. One was bright, obviously working to keep the walls in place. But the boy had two more, both sparkling though not currently active.

There was something odd about the light in the room as well. The walls were shifting through several colours which was reasonable, as it made them stronger. But now that Tal looked at them he realised that the overall colour in the room was a sickly grey. No normal Chosen ever used that colour.

Tal raised his hand and bright white flashed out flooding every corner of the room.

In its stark illumination Tal saw that Lenan was not really Lenan. The Chosen boy was just a picture woven from light masking something much larger. An only approximately human thing of rotting flesh and naked bone that rose up and cast its disguise away.

Hazror.

The three Sunstones Lenan had worn were not an illusion. Hazror picked one up in a hand that was more claw than anything else. Light flickered in the stone building in intensity.

Tal didn't wait for whatever Hazror was going to do. He changed the light in his Sunstone from white to red and sent a Red Ray of Destruction blasting out at Hazror's head.

Hazror countered with a Violet Shield of Discontinuity and the Red Ray disappeared into some other, unknown reality. But the Shield only covered his head. Blasting off another ray at his enemy's knees Tal dove to the ground.

That saved his life. Hazror instantly counterattacked and a great blast of Indigo light flashed over Tal's head. Tal didn't even know what the spell was, except that it was enormously destructive.

His Red Ray hit Hazror, but several hidden Sunstones flashed around his calves, absorbing the strike. Other stones glittered into life along his arms and thighs.

Tal gasped in shock as an aura of light sprang up all round the creature.

Hazror was literally covered in Sunstones. Hundreds and hundreds of them.

With so many defensive Sunstones Tal's light attacks were useless.

Hazror was invulnerable...